ADVANCE P'

"A well-crafted novella of startling relationships that dares the reader to reinterpret love and lust . . . [a tale] beautifully intertwined with the fervor of music."
—REBECCA SWANEY, *Adventures in Reading*

"An author's glance into the twilight of maturing years . . . a story that will astound you. Witness the dance."
—LARRY BULLOUGH, Advance Reader

"*We Are DNA* stands as a testament to Lucas's honed craft. . . . [The story's] powerful prose and intense use of imagery make even the most conservative reader find sympathy with its disturbed protagonist. If you were drawn into *The Boy with Black Eyes*, prepare to be blown away by *We Are DNA*."
—DANIEL WILLIAMS, Advance Reader

"*We Are DNA* will have you squirming in your chair, laughing out loud, and running your mascara—just maybe not in that order."
—MELISSA GRANT, Advance Reader

"A modern-day *Lolita* with a far more feasible plot. Unlike Nabokov's tale, I can actually envision this one happening in the real-world."
—JESSE DILLON, Advance Reader

"I have a new favorite author."
—CHRIS WRIGHT, Advance Reader

ALSO BY BRIAN LUCAS
The Boy with Black Eyes

we are DNA

a novella

brian lucas

PANIC
P R E S S

FIRST PAPERBACK EDITION, FEBRUARY 2009

Copyright © 2008-2009 by Brian Lucas

All rights reserved, including the right to reproduce this book or portions thereof in any form whatsoever. For information address PANIC Press, 6985 Thornwood Street NW, Canton, OH 44718.

Library of Congress Cataloging-in-Publication Data
Lucas, Brian
We Are DNA/Brian Lucas.—1st paperback ed.
p.   cm.
ISBN-10: 0-9814879-2-0
ISBN-13: 978-0-9814879-2-2
1. Piano—Fiction. 2. Marriage—Fiction. 3. Middle age—Fiction. 4. Taboo—Fiction. 5. Romance—Fiction. 6. Midwest States—Fiction. 7. Akron (Oh.)—Fiction. I. Title.

For information about special discounts for bulk purchases, please contact PANIC Press Sales at sales@brian-lucas.com.

Set in Adobe Caslon
Book design by Brian Lucas

www.brian-lucas.com/dna

This book is a work of fiction. Names, characters, places, incidents, and episodes either are products of the author's imagination or are used fictitiously. Any resemblance to actual events or locales or persons, living or dead, is entirely coincidental.

The scanning, uploading, and distribution of this book via the Internet or via any other means without the permission of the publisher is illegal and punishable by law. Please purchase only authorized electronic editions and digital reproductions, and do not engage in or support online piracy of copyrighted print materials. Your support of the author's rights and livelihood is appreciated.

Printed in the United States of America
10   9   8   7   6   5   4   3   2   1

To Bunga with love eternal and admiration true

The tragedy of it is that nobody sees the look of desperation on my face. Thousands and thousands of us, and we're passing one another without a look of recognition.

—HENRY MILLER, *Black Spring*

we are
DNA

Inspired by true events

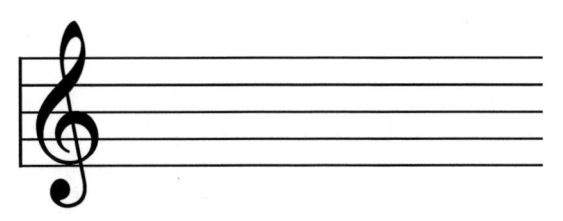

You wake up at the same time in the same way. Nine o'clock in the morning, cuckoo clocks and chamomile. You look outside. Another gray sky. No surprise. Autumns in Ohio are bleak as hell. You should know this. You've lived here for the whole of your life—what is it now, fifty-seven years? Well, fifty-eight, but who's counting? Certainly not Mrs. Kuhn. She has been up since five, and lord only knows what she has already accomplished by this hour.

Lifting your head from your pillow, you smell the sickeningly sweet, yet pungent, odor of white tea. And that's exactly what it is—an odor. Not a fragrance, not a scent, and goddamn it, definitely not a perfume. There's no need to check the nightstand; you know what's there. A once clear, now cloudy, mug of Shinto White Tea. What makes it "Shinto" you'll never know. You've never cared enough to inspect the box in which it's purchased, the cardboard cache stored in the downstairs kitchen closet from which Mrs. Kuhn takes two bags a day—one for you, one for her—and steeps them to gross imperfection.

You've never liked white tea; you've made this known time and time again. There was a time when your opinion mattered. Many years ago, for about a week, she switched to green, a Chinese blend infused with orange citrus. You appreciated the change. You made this known. Despite your gratitude, however, the green tea didn't last long. Six days later, white made its triumphant return. Mrs. Kuhn claimed the grocer's green tea supplies depleted, that the store had discontinued the product line. That morning you had a banana. Throwing away the peel, you discovered twelve bags of citrus-infused green in the trash, all of which were dry, unused. You never mentioned this to Mrs. Kuhn, never again complained about her tea preferences. Every morning, the present included, a cup lies waiting, and every morning the sink drinks its contents. Routine—fixed, immobile.

You have just under an hour to get ready, and despite the comfiness of your down comforter, you mustn't delay. The master bathroom's stone tile, as usual, is relentlessly cold. Your feet sting as you hop toward the oaken closet and pull a monographed towel from the stack. "HK." You

we are dna

consciously avoid those linens bearing your wife's initials: "TK," Tabitha Kuhn. Last October, you absentmindedly dried your face with a washcloth identified as hers. She reacted violently. Like the green tea, the hand towel hit the trash. That night, a memo (on monogrammed stationery, no less) appeared on your bed pillow. Penned in her finest calligraphy, it read:

> Mr. Kuhn —
> Please select your fineries with utmost care and caution. This morrow, you soiled an article of a third party's possession. I tried to salvage it, but alas, 'twas of no use. I'll purchase a replacement in the upcoming days. I sorely hope this addressing of the matter sufficient.
> Regards,
> T. Kuhn

Her script was immaculate. Not a single curve, a single stroke was malformed. You wondered just how many times this note was rewritten, how much stationery was destroyed because of an ill-executed "f," an imperfect "p." You hated how she felt compelled to draft a formal grievance, how she couldn't simply confront the issue in daily conversation. But more than that, you hated her haughtiness, how it was so amply revealed in her archaic word choice. Morrow? 'Twas? You have been married for thirty-six years. The woman who sleeps beside you is not your wife, is not your lover, is not even a companion. She is just a body, a cold one at that.

Taking a shower doesn't stir your spirits. Like your wife's embrace and the tile's touch, it is too frigid to bear. Your house is a turn-of-the-century Tudor, too medieval for your liking. Its pipes haven't pumped hot water since 1928. Skin crawling with goose bumps, you wipe yourself dry. Your skin, your hair smell of lye soap, another of your wife's neuroses. Her delicate complexion can't handle fine beauty products with their all-natural ingredients and earthy scents. Even perfume-free shampoos are rumored to cause pus-laden reactions. So like her antebellum ancestors, she (and by extension, you) use good ole-fashioned Gramma's Choice Lye. Anything else will apparently shatter what she calls her "porcelain skin." You've never understood that analogy. After all, porcelain doesn't blotch or flake. You've seen your wife do both.

Saturdays are teaching days, and as a result, you dress yourself accordingly. You are of the belief that modesty, like wisdom, should only increase with age. Men over fifty should never, under any condition, expose their legs or bare chests to the general public. It's just something you don't do. No one revels in the pallor of your sagging thighs, in

we are dna

the curiously wire-like quality of your chest hair. There's really no need to subject the world to such an unpalatable sight. No, you are a man of grace, of refinement, but above all, of tact. Brown or black trousers with a button-down dress shirt; no plaid unless posing as a forest ranger. The shirt should be buttoned close to the neck and tucked in, a belt securing this arrangement. Always wear shoes. Bare feet, even youthful, supple ones, are prone to inspire disgust. Wearing only socks is much too informal, too casual for a man posing as an authority figure. Cologne is welcome as long as it is subtle, discreet. Never select a fragrance that smells of bark, timber, spruce, or pine. These are the perfumes of a forest, not of a dignified intellectual. You spritz yourself by an open window, with the overhead fan on. If Mrs. Kuhn should encounter any sort of lingering aroma, you'll hear about it for days. Well, not so much hear as read. A placard would be delivered to your pillow, affixed to your dresser.

Your house's spiral staircase is grandiose, opulent in the extreme. As you clomp down and around it, you can't help but feel as though you're involved in some sort of awards ceremony, a guest presenter making your entrance. The piece was imported from Paris, an architectural masterpiece gutted from some opera house, a holdover from the gilded age, no doubt. It was Mrs. Kuhn's doing, was bought on holiday in Europe. You weren't invited to join her, though, to be fair, you probably wouldn't have gone even if asked. Daddy Dukes financed the six-week excursion. He financed just about every noteworthy expense of your married life—this house, its furnishings, the Benz, even Tabitha's wedding ring. You had no choice in the matter. As Dukes had explained, your "paltry income" could never provide for his daughter what she duly deserved.

As your feet hit the hardwood floor, Mrs. Kuhn appears to be waiting for you in the grand hall. She's idling by the door to the salon, her hair stringier than usual, her dress dull and shapeless. If she were thirty years younger, she might be confused for a waif. Age, however, has rendered that moniker obsolete; at fifty-nine, she's more tragic than even the lowliest of waifs.

Her eyes meet yours. You smile; she remains dispassionate.

"Your ten o'clock is here, Mr. Kuhn," she announces, gaze dropping to the floor.

"Ah, very good, right on time," you say, traipsing into the kitchen. "Did you get their names?"

"No, I have yet to greet them. The door chime just sounded. Didn't you hear it?"

"Obviously not," you reply, trying to stifle your annoyance. Why must she always insist upon using uncommon language? You have a door *bell* and it *rings*. For the

we are dna

love of God, she acts as though colloquial phrases are beneath her, that the language of the masses isn't good enough, sophisticated enough for her.

You scan the calendar on the fridge for today's date: Saturday, September 26. In red pen you've written, "Katherine Merriden and Brandine. 10 AM."

Returning to the hall, you then hurry to the front door, checking your zipper as you go. There's no better way to scare off potential students than to greet them with your pants open.

"C'mon, Mrs. Kuhn," you encourage, "you've got to say hello too."

"Oh? For what reason?" She remains where she is, defiantly, hands crossed over her nonexistent bosom.

"You know why. Now c'mon, before they ring again or think we aren't home!"

Years ago, you made this a policy—that whenever new students arrive, both you and Mrs. Kuhn alike introduce yourselves. Most parents are already overprotective of their children. No reason to make them more so by appearing a spouseless recluse with an affinity for youngsters. You've learned that mere mention of a wife isn't evidence enough. Most want a face in addition to a name. It was only then that their labeling you a pervert would cease. Though you hated this formality almost as much as Mrs. Kuhn, it had become a necessary evil, one to which you both routinely submitted.

Begrudgingly, Mrs. Kuhn joins you at the door. In flipping the deadbolt and depressing a lever, you let morning creak into the corridor, slowly, languidly.

"Well, good morning!" you greet, popping a smile as unnatural as your wife's preoccupation with white tea. "You must be Ms. Merriden and Brandine, right? Please do come in."

A Maybellined mom and child clack over the threshold and onto the hallway's recently polished hardwood floor. They are wearing identical black-and-white dresses—very *Pilgrim's Progress*—with onyx hose and piercingly white stilettos. The middle-aged parent and/or guardian (one can never be sure) is sporting a surgically enhanced face, the scars still slightly visible, and an eau de toilette so strong that it burns the nasal passages. You instantly know what's coming. There's no way to avoid it, no means by which to suppress it. In moments such as these, you've learned to embrace the short-term embarrassment, then let it pass. You stand silently and wait.

As if by a director's cue, she starts.

"Oh, dear heavens, what is that god-awful stench?!"

Mrs. Kuhn's hands are flailing about her face. Squinting her eyes shut, she wrinkles her nose in repulsion. "Christ's mercy, Christ's mercy!" she begins to screech, her head bobbing back and forth as though in some sort of

we are dna

trance.

At this your guests are visibly distressed. The woman's maternal instinct tells her to shield the child from danger. She pulls the young girl behind her back.

"Is e-e-everything all right?" the woman stutters, face growing flush. "Is it my perfume?"

Mrs. Kuhn stops swaying and instead opens her eyes to the brink of bulging.

"Perfume? Perfume! Is that what you call it?!" Tabitha screams, a string of spittle dangling from her mouth. "The smell of the devil's entrails, that's what it is! Bloody hell!"

"Tabitha!" you interject, your wife always going one step too far. "Enough!" You turn her around toward the kitchen, murmuring in her ear, "Now you go back to the sink and flush your eyes. Take a few deep breaths. Have a glass of water. Do whatever it takes to calm down."

Mrs. Kuhn looks up at you, her eyes red and wet. She appears an utter mess, her skin beginning to welt, eyes twitching. Maybe she wasn't overreacting. Maybe she really is allergic to strong dyes and perfumes. Regardless, you don't have time to figure it out just now. You send her off with a gentle squeeze of her shoulder. As she begins her retreat galleyward, you think that you hear her grumble something. No, she definitely *is* grumbling something. Over and over again, repeating the words.

brian lucas

"Smelly slut."

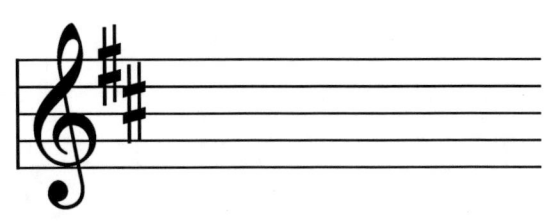

It takes several minutes to fully explain the incident to the disgruntled pair of Puritans Gone Wild. You ask them if they'd like to remove their six-inch stilettos. They decline. You invite them into the parlor for a short pre-session briefing.

Every new parent and student is given the same baseline lecture. You've said it so many times over the years that it has become second nature. In fact, you've reached the point where you don't even think about the words. They just spill out. Instead, you focus your attention on other things, like the colony of dust bunnies in the far corner of the room or that curiously colored mole on the woman's face. You don't really make an effort to infuse inflection into your voice. They'll either listen or they won't.

brian lucas

You've been a piano instructor for five years, ever since you resigned from Elmwood High, the school at which you taught geography and conducted band. Your years there were nothing short of sublime. Retiring was difficult. Your wife is Tabitha Kuhn, and you've been married for thirty-six years. They haven't been happy years, but, well, you don't really get into that. You received your undergraduate degree in music theory and practice at Baldwin-Wallace College. Your master's came from the University of Akron, in education. You play the oboe, clarinet, and bassoon in addition to the piano. You've performed with the Cleveland Symphony Orchestra. In your free time you like to write music and watch the BBC. Even though no one really cares about your interests, you feel the need to share.

Lessons are fixed-rate, thirty dollars per forty-five-minute session. Payment is expected at the time of instruction. The fee includes all supplementary materials and sheet music. You no longer accept retroactive payments, not even the occasional IOU. You've been burned too many times. No check, cash, or money order, no lesson. Credit cards are not a valid form of payment. They are too much bother, require too much machinery and too much personal information to be "secure." You request forgiveness for the harshness of your policies. You ask that they understand where you're coming from, that there are too

we are dna

many unscrupulous people in the world.

You give lessons six days a week, every day except the one on which most people, including Mrs. Kuhn, make a deal with God. Since playing the piano is a recreational hobby, you want your students to enjoy their sessions. As a result, you encourage their visiting as frequently or infrequently as they like. A few students come as often as three times a week. You assume this is not the students' preference but instead that of their bossy parents. Many take lessons once a week or twice a month. You endeavor to remind parents that more lessons do not inherently guarantee faster results. Students, regardless of the subject, learn at their own pace. We must accept this.

You look at Brandine. She appears attentive but is indubitably bored. Her hands are clasped, resting upon her left thigh. Having likely suffered through some sort of finishing-school crash course, she sits upright, with her feet on the floor, ankles crossed. Her mom, for reasons unknown, is beaming.

"Well, Brandine, now that you're ready for a nap," you jest, winking at the girl, "let's get to a more important matter." The mother's glow suddenly goes dark. She sits up in her chair, her expression oddly grave. Uneasily, you continue. "What makes you want to play the piano?"

The mom looks confused, quasi-annoyed. You decide to elaborate. "What I mean is, why do you want to take lessons?"

No good. No change in Mother Goose; she is still just as distraught as before.

"Let me put it this way: What are you looking for from our time together?"

Brandine's expression is warm, receptive. The mother, you reason, would rather have her purse stolen than endure this conversation. Brandine licks her lips and clears her throat. Calmly, she opens her mouth.

"Well, Mom told me—"

"What she means to say," Ms. Merriden interrupts, shooting a frown at Brandine, "is that ... well, Mr. Kuhn, to be honest, she loves everything. She loves pressing the keys, hearing the hammers, heck, even rubbing her feet on the pedals." Her shoulders back, she puffs out her chest with pride, a shrewd interviewee having averted a pitfall.

"I see," you say, knowing the mom a liar. "And for just how long have you been playing, *Brandine?*" You drop the name hard, as if it were a priceless vase and you a destructive child. Eyes fixed on the girl, you invite her into the conversation.

"I'd say about two years," the mom guesses, nodding slowly.

Brandine whips her head around and stares at her mom. The girl's mouth is ajar, her eyebrows raised. Ms. Merriden pretends not to notice. She wiggles her wrist,

we are dna

freeing a bracelet that was caught in her arm hair.

"You know, give or take," she adds; it's a fumbled recovery. "To be honest, it seems to me as if she's been playing forever. She's always, um, what is that phrase, 'teething the ivories'?"

"It's 'tickling,'" you correct, "but I know what you mean."

"Yes, well, I say 'toothing,' you say 'tickling.' It's like tomato, tomahto, right?" This attempt at a joke amuses her, and she chuckles to herself.

You, on the other hand, want her out of your house. Now.

"Brandine, how old are you, hon?" *Jesus God*, you think, *let her answer this one for herself.*

"She's twelve."

Ms. Merriden might be aggressive, your brain buzzes, *but ignorant she is not.*

You don't do children. That's how it's always been said; Mr. Kuhn doesn't "do children." And it's true. After all, you went into secondary education for a reason, had no children for a reason. They annoy you. Always have, always will.

Besides, you aren't teaching piano for the money. It's a pastime. Pastimes are supposed to be fun. You don't have fun when a child is present; is crying; is pooping; hell, is giggling. Never have, never will. Being a paid contractor, age discrimination is within your legal authority. Eleven and up. No exceptions.

At the moment, however, you feel as though the adoption of another clause is due. No overbearing parents. No exceptions. Later tonight, you may or may not share a laugh with your wife about this, depending on her mood. Mrs. Kuhn, you've come to learn, is as unpredictable as the weather (and that's with or without Doppler equipment; there's really no difference).

Hoisting yourself out of your seat, you move toward the far wall, toward the piano. This, in effect, ends your call-and-response game with Ms. Merriden. There's no clear winner. It's a draw.

You flip a switch, and the piano's lamp flickers to life. Its luminescence, however, is anything but inviting. So cold is the light that the sheet music propped just below appears a soft blue. It reminds you of the fat-free, flavor-free, and practically lactose-free skim milk enjoyed by Mrs. Kuhn. You cringe as you think about her gulping down a glass of the watery paste.

Lifting the keyboard cover up and then back, you reveal the elephant tusks housed just below. They too appear a creamy cerulean. You look back at Brandine to request her accompaniment. Her eyes are terrified. Something about her—maybe it's the way she's trembling—tells you that she isn't the piano virtuoso her mother proclaims her

we are dna

to be. Still, she is here for a lesson, so a lesson she shall have. You smile as warmly as you can in the cool light.

"Brandine, before I can begin teaching you something new, I need to measure your current skill level; that's how I'll know where to proceed from. Why don't you come on over here, and we'll get started."

Tentatively, the girl approaches the hardwood bench. Her mother once again appears irritated but stays where she is and, for the first time, says nothing. Her arms are crossed over her cleavage. As you rise from the bench, Brandine in turn flops down, scooting herself along the pillow to its center. There she awaits further instruction.

Never one to invade a child's personal space, especially when a high-strung parent is present, you squat down near the stiff seat and run your fingers through your hair.

"Brandine, do you know how to sight-read music?" You breathe the question so softly that it could be mistaken for a purr. More than anything, you want Brandine, and only Brandine, to respond, to speak her mind in her very own voice. You want her to feel as though she can be open with you, candid. You want her not to worry what her mother thinks.

Just as Brandine seems to begin to shake her head, her mother pipes in.

"Excuse me, Mr. Kuhn, but what did you say? I couldn't hear you from way back here. Either that or you're whispering."

At a distance, Ms. Merriden is not so attractive. She is seated with rigid posture in an easy chair; the veins running down her neck are thick and turgid. Her nose seems somewhat flat and her ears too big, her gullet too puffy. Up close, she has the marks of a prom queen—an aged, somewhat unpleasant prom queen, but a prom queen nevertheless. From afar, she's rather piggish.

"Ms. Merriden, I was just asking your daughter whether or not she has learned how to sight-read music."

The swine bats her eyelashes in disbelief.

"My God, Mr. Kuhn, my Brandine has been doing that since she was—Jesus—like eight." She expels a bitter huff. "Forgive me, but I uh, well, I find it a bit insulting that you'd think her incapable of such an elementary skill. Perhaps one of your inner-city pupils would find such a baseline task challenging, but, well, Brandine is of a different class. I'll have you know she underwent extensive IQ testing last autumn and has been certified by the state of Ohio as academically gifted."

So few parents or, for that matter, people in general realize that their getting defensive is a sign of weakness and vulnerability, not strength. Those who are genuinely capable—that is, those who possess real talent or ability—seldom mind being misjudged, wrongly critiqued. These individuals know themselves exceptional regardless of what

we are dna

this person may say or that person may think. Should it be deemed necessary, they could always prove their prowess, demonstrate their dexterity. Only those who are loose in their convictions, who are lacking in self-confidence, take offense in times such as these. You know this to be true. You've seen it play out time after time in classroom after classroom. You ask a student if he or she is proficient in world geography. The student is shocked and dismayed, "can't believe you would even ask that." A week later, this same student struggles to name America's fifty states, to identify Texas on a map. He or she then goes on to fail your exam.

"No offense, Ms. Merriden, but my question was directed at Brandine. Unless there's some sort of logical reason why she cannot answer for herself, I'd appreciate it if you'd be so kind as to stop interrupting my instruction. I ask this not for my own benefit but for Brandine's. You must understand my dilemma here; how am I to teach your daughter if I can't even speak to her?"

You've had just about enough of Ms. Merriden, and frankly, you don't care if she knows it. As much as you'd rather not embarrass Brandine, this woman needs to be put in her place, needs to know that her constant intervention isn't appropriate. You don't need her money, and you definitely don't need her arrogance. If she got up and left right now, voiceless daughter in hand, it wouldn't be too soon.

brian lucas

Instead, however, she stays where she is and, to your surprise, shrinks back in her chair.

"Forgive me, I … well, I just don't know what has gotten into me." She looks down at the floor, scratches a heavily rouged cheek. "I guess I just know Brandine is an extraordinary girl, you know?" Weakly, she grins at the uncomfortable preteen who, in knowing not what to do, has literally begun to twiddle her thumbs. "I hate it when people don't see her potential, that's all." She shifts her gaze over to you, explores your face for what she hopes to be a wrinkle of clemency, jowl of sympathy. These are age marks, emotions she has long since done away with, characteristics which were dismissed as inferior, base, of a race to which she doesn't belong. The woman doesn't see herself, her glorious Brandine, as being human. No, surely they are above that.

You ask Brandine to move aside for a moment as you lift open the seat of the bench. Inside is a sepulcher of sheet music, the songs and arrangements so old, so yellowed that they are no longer intellectual property but instead, un-prized pieces of the public domain. You grab a red songbook—its cover half decayed—entitled *Whimsies for All Seasons*. Inside is a one-handed composition, "Dicks and Donnas," which you think a good starter piece for Brandine to attempt. It's a simple tune, just a half page in length, with plenty of repetition and rests. Perfect for be-

we are dna

ginners. You flop it up against the piano's music rack and invite Brandine to once again take her place on the padded bench.

"All right, hon, now this is, admittedly, a very basic piece. It involves only, what, let's see here"—you count the notes—"hm, just five piano keys. A, B, Middle-C, D, and E. No big deal, right?"

You glance over at Brandine. The color has left her face. She looks—no, she most definitely *is*—petrified. That being said, she maintains her composure. Blinking anxiously, she curves her mouth into what, under normal circumstances, would be called a smile. It isn't one, though. Smiles express amusement, and Brandine, with her ghoulish complexion, seems anything but amused. Still, she is her mother's child; what she doesn't know, she'll fake.

"No, Mr. Kuhn," she squeaks, "you got that right. Easy as pie."

The girl looks up at the musical notation, then back down at the keys. The first note is an F. It is to be held for four beats. Brandine doesn't know this. When she looks at the grand staff, all she sees is an oval trapped between two lines. She has no idea what this corresponds to or, worse, how it even relates to the eighty-eight keys before her. Nervously, she extends her middle finger and, in taking a wild guess, presses a white key. She plays a D, the wrong note. She turns to you for feedback.

You want to stop her, to tell her that it's all right, that the two of you will start from the very beginning, that you'll take it one step at a time. Her mother, however, has something else in mind.

"Brandine," Ms. Merriden scolds, her throat sounding dry, coarse, "just what do you think you're doing?! Now stop your fooling around, and play the song for the man!"

The girl returns her gaze to the sheet music. Reading left to right, the next symbol she must tackle is another oval, this one having been impaled, skewered, on a line. It's a C. This time, Brandine chooses a black key. She plays an F sharp. Eyes to the sheet music, she encounters still another oval, this one between the very same lines as the first. It's another F. Forgetting which key she had originally selected, she picks one at random. An E.

You turn and look at Ms. Merriden. She's checking her watch. In lifting her head, she shrugs her shoulders, as if to say, "Don't look at me; she's never played like this before." Standing in silence, you watch as Brandine forces down another five keys. An A, a G, a C sharp, a B, and a D. All arbitrary selections, all wrong ones at that. The tension in the air is tightening, becoming more and more palpable. Ms. Merriden must have felt it. She stands up, straightens her dress, and walks, one foot in front of the

we are dna

other, over to the piano. She rests her hands on her child's shoulders.

"Could you excuse us for a moment, Mr. Kuhn?" she asks. "If it's all right with you, I'd like to have a word with my daughter." Gently pulling Brandine's hair back behind her ears, she strokes it softly. Her eight-carat diamond ring glitters in the waves of her child's cinnamon sea.

Politely, you acquiesce to her request, walking across the room to your desk in the opposite corner. There you pretend to review a credit card statement from two Christmases ago while, in your peripheral vision, you watch that which you promised to ignore.

Brandine has turned around on the bench and is facing her parent. You eye the colorless blur that is her mother as she drops to her knees and, with hands outstretched, grabs her daughter by the shoulders. She speaks in a tone much louder than was likely intended.

"What the *hell* do you think you're doing, you little piss-rat?!" she hisses, digging her nails into the child's bony arms. "I brought you all the way out here, am paying thirty fucking dollars, and for what? For you to sheepishly stroke the wrong goddamn keys?! What has gotten into you?!"

There's something glistening on Brandine's cheeks. You assume it to be tears.

"Mom," you hear her cry, "I don't know how to sight-read! The two songs I know—those ones that Jeremy taught me—I learned by memorizing. I have no idea what these circles and lines are supposed to mean!"

"Listen here, you little twit," Ms. Merriden rails, "you better learn and learn *fast*. God, by the time she was your age, Kerri was already sucking the hell out of that bassoon of hers. You remember how she'd suck that thing dry? Well, do you?!"

She shakes the girl violently. The sparkles on Brandine's cheeks increase in size, in number.

"Yes, Mom, I remember," the girl confesses, lowering her head, "but I'm not Kerri. I'm my own person, and Mrs. Darkoe told me there's nothing wrong with that."

At this the mom clutches the girl's face, pulls it up toward hers.

"Yes, Brandine, you're right; you are your own person. And do you know who that person is?" She pauses a minute for dramatic effect. "An utter failure."

Ms. Merriden cranes her neck. Her nose is nearly touching Brandine's.

"You listen to me, and you listen good. You are a disgrace to this family. You are"—and she says these next words slowly, with diction—"mor-ti-fy-ing me."

You shut your eyes. For a moment, you are no longer Mr. Kuhn, the piano teacher, the man of a sexless marriage, but Harry the Fairy, a child of eight, the pride of your mother, shame of your father. You were his

we are dna

Brandine; he was your Ms. Merriden. So forcefully would he cradle your face in his hands that you often feared your jaw might break. He'd stare at you with those cold, resentful eyes, those balls of blue ice, those immutable stones to which love, affection proved impervious. The odor of his hatred was so strong, so concentrated that a single whiff would render your body limp and your mind empty. He'd spit the words into your eyes, chisel them into your soul. "You *will* play a sport. You *will* like it."

It's not as if you didn't try to impress him, didn't try to jump through his ever higher and smaller hoops. It's just that whenever you'd finally begin to enjoy a given sport, begin to achieve modest success, he'd give you reason not only to resent the game but also yourself. You liked volleyball and badminton, but little did you know, "net sports are for wimps and homosexuals." When croquet and bocce ball caught your interest, you unknowingly caught something else: his critical eye. They were, after all, "more pansy sports" invented by "aristocrats and ugly, impotent Limeys." As a teenager, you'd attempt your final two athletic endeavors: track and lacrosse. To be honest, you weren't particularly interested in either but participated only to appease your father, something which, in the end, you of course failed to do. Track, you see, was designed specifically for "latent homosexuals." Why else would you get down on all fours at the beginning of a race? It doesn't

brian lucas

help you spring into a sprint. It's nothing more than a good position in which to "be sodomized." And lacrosse? Hell, with all that physical contact and talk of balls and sticks, you might as well just cut to the chase and "faggot one another" (he'd often verbify the pejorative noun).

The asshole died of a coronary at the age of fifty-nine. You were thirty-two at the time and the one your family had expected to make the necessary funeral arrangements. You gave him a decent but forgettable funeral, his casket without embellishments, the specified sermons uninspired. When the time came for the thirty or so guests to say their final goodbyes, they formed a line and approached the corpse one by one. Some genuflected, others made a sign of the cross, but most family members kissed his forehead. You were second to last in line. As you crossed the threshold, you felt the weight of those present, their expectations, pressing down on your shoulders. At funerals, people want to see sadness, see tears, see the very fabric of life shed for those who are dead. By this time, your mom, brother, and sisters were, collectively, a red, salty mess. The shag carpet crunched under your feet. You had a choice; you could either concede to the desires of others, stage a spectacle, or be who you are, a wilted, resentful shred of humanity, and act accordingly. You neared the deathbed. You steadied your gait and shut your eyes. You didn't kiss him on the forehead, didn't pause, bow, didn't

we are dna

even look in his direction. You turned the corner and, stepping blindly, in faith, excused yourself from the ceremony, walked out the door. You never shed a tear. You never looked back.

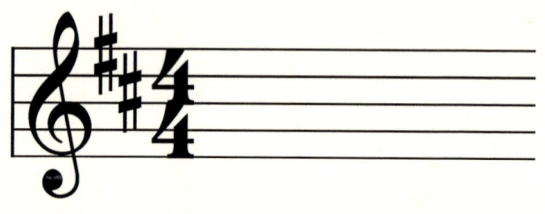

Brandine and her mother leave at ten-thirty that morning. You couldn't care less. You know that they'll never return, that you'll never see them again. Brandine's hands may never again touch a piano, may never again ask to hold her mother's. You wish that there was something you could do or say to make right all of Ms. Merriden's past and future wrongs. You know such a thing doesn't exist. Standing in your study, you exhale; you let Brandine's fledgling spirit go. You're too old, too weak to meddle in other people's business. You've done so in the past and it's made little difference. Since then, you've evolved beyond the delusion that one person's capable of entirely changing the world. You have narrowed your horizons, drawn them not miles but meters away. You've stopped believing in God, stopped trusting in faith, and

we are dna

believe yourself better off for it.

You often contemplate suicide. You do so without a sense of urgency, without a hunger for an end but rather a protracted tiredness of the present. You've never felt more wearied with life, with its tedium and monotony, than you do now. In months and years past, you saw a reason for life, a purpose in pulling yourself off the bed. The days held enormous prospect and possibility. They no longer retain that depth, that density. Something has most certainly changed in either you or your world. Probably both. In truth, you care not what it is. You are almost sixty years old. Your decay of mind, body, and spirit is inevitable, imminent even. Just as well that it happens today as opposed to tomorrow. Less time to wait, to anticipate the fall.

You spend the remainder of your day at leisure, doing those things which you *almost* seem to enjoy. You take a nap, watch a British soap, listen to your wife touch herself in the bathroom. You haven't had an erection in months, had sex in over a decade. Tabitha's god, one of Calvinist design, tells her that intimacy serves but one purpose—namely, procreation, the peopling of the Earth. Once your aversion to children was declassified, Tabitha began actively refusing sexual activity.

Demonstrating her strict adherence to dogma, she'd brandish her centuries-old Bible, and, with her index finger raised, her lumpy nightie bearing witness, she'd speak of divine providence. "We are to run, Harold," she would proclaim, her eyes wet and lips dry. "Yes, we are to run from anything that stimulates youthful lust. Timothy, chapter two." Clumsily she'd thumb through the pages, dig deeper into the work. She'd clear her throat.

"Then each of you will control your body and live in holiness and honor, not in lustful passion as the pagans do. No, for mercy's sake, we mustn't emulate their abominable example. Do you hear this, Harold? Do you hear Christ's word as revealed in Thessalonians, chapter four? It's all here, everything you'd want to know, all here, codified and made forever accessible, if only we'd listen." She would then nod, as if reaffirming to herself this notion.

These performances, these grandiose readings, they went on for days. In time, you surrendered to her stubborn will. You feigned a second birth, a transcendental moment of epiphany. You accepted her word as Truth, told her you found your libido repulsive, that you wanted to free your soul from the torment of your fiery, tempestuous loins. In reality, you kind of looked forward to the return of masturbation, the reunion of your hand with your penis. After all, sex with Tabitha was never much of a treat. On your honeymoon, the lovemaking, while not great, was at least tepid, lukewarm, like the water in a bathtub after twenty minutes of bathing. Now take that same bathwater and imagine its being cooled then drained from the tub. That

we are dna

was sex with middle-aged Tabitha; a largely dry, thoroughly chilly affair.

Never once in your thirty-six years of marriage did she moan or groan, communicate to you her body's experiencing pleasure. Year after year, tryst after tryst, there was no change in her attitude, her behavior. You'd tell her to relax, to lie back and enjoy the experience. She'd have no such thing. Her body would actively refuse you. You'd ask her if you could remove her panties, if you could put your mouth where they'd regularly sit. She'd tell you, "Don't be sick," would lift the briefs up higher, pull them tighter. You'd tell her of your simple fantasies, that she would allow you to do with her what you will, that she'd permit your routine occupation of her kingdom. She'd respond with a glare, then request that you sleep on the couch.

It was actually during one of your many nights on the couch that you first learned of Mrs. Kuhn's affinity for self-love. The house was quiet, still. You were sound asleep, slobbering on the throw pillows, when the thumping began. The sound was loud, its vibration rhythmic. The clamor reminded you of something one might hear in a factory, the bang-bang-bang of a piston being fired, perhaps. It was coming from the second floor. Groggy-eyed and drowsy, you climbed the stairs and, upon reaching the landing, stopped. The ruckus persisted, unabated. Bang-bang-bang-bang. You could now identify the sound; it was the creaking of the floorboards. Only, they weren't so much creaking as they were breaking, splintering. You walked toward the master bedroom. The door was open. The sound grew louder. Though the room was dark, a sliver of light shone forth from the adjoining bathroom. Its door was cracked open. You slinked forward and, in aligning your left eye with the slit, peeked inside.

Squatted down on the floor, naked, looking in the opposite direction, was Mrs. Kuhn. For a moment or two, you weren't exactly sure what she was doing. It was an unusual position to be sure, one in which you'd never seen her before—well, that isn't exactly true. A week or so prior, you had accidentally dropped a champagne flute from a high-flying kitchen cabinet, one which, for reasons unknown, nearly touches the ceiling. By the time you located the dustpan and broom (in the pantry, behind the potato chips), Tabitha was already down on her haunches, collecting the shards. She was using her bare hands.

Days later, when you spied her in the bathroom, her pose was virtually unchanged. Only this time there was no glass to sweep, no debris to gather. Nothing lay broken in front of her; nothing stood damaged by her feet or crumpled near her exposed buttocks. Still, her hands were busy. What could she be doing with them? What purpose could such a movement have? Then you understood. She was doing that which so many do but so few talk about. You

we are dna

wondered just how long this had been going on, if it were the reason why she no longer desired your touch, your patented caress.

That next day, you threw away your condoms. You visited an adult video store and purchased a variety of titles—gay, straight, and bisexual alike. From that day forward, you'd keep the Sabbath holy in your own way—in your private quarters, with the door shut, lock engaged, and your hands and body on anything and everything except another person. Your marriage would be sexless, no doubt, but that didn't mean you couldn't explore your sexuality in other ways or with other things. Just not people.

The euphoria that is your Sunday ends abruptly with a turn of a knob, the swoosh of a slip-on. In walks Mrs. Kuhn clad in a velour gown complete with turtleneck and a new pair of plastic flats. Sad to say, this absolute disaster is your wife at her most attractive, in her Sunday best. She often brags to her fellow parishioners about her frugality, how her dress has survived the 80s, 90s, and today, how her sandals cost only cents on the dollar. She believes her thrifty fashion sense unerring. Most, you reason, would beg to differ.

Despite the fact that mass lets out at noon, Tabitha seldom arrives home before five-thirty. You know not how she spends her day. You've inquired in the past. You've gotten nowhere.

She swooshes down the hall and into your study.

we are dna

You're standing before the copying machine, reproducing sheet music for tomorrow's lessons. She taps on your back with something hard, something round. You glance back, catching a glimpse of a red lollipop.

"Whatcha got there?" you ask, pressing the COPY button. A bar of lime light passes over your document. A reproduction of "Nancy's Plaything" falls into the tray.

"Oh, I haven't any idea," Mrs. Kuhn jokes, tapping the shrink-wrapped confection against her head. "Whatever does it look like?"

You lift the machine's lid, replacing one piece of music with another. You hit COPY. "Looks to me like someone went trick-or-treating on her way home from church."

Mrs. Kuhn snorts. You don't know if that's a good thing or a bad thing. Thankfully, you're too preoccupied to ponder the significance. The emerald light reappears. A freshly inked sheet of paper drops to the tray.

"No, actually, but that reminds me," she says, her fingers struggling against the plastic wrap, "I better seek out our All Hallows' Eve decorations. They're haunting our attic at the moment, I do believe."

You hear what sounds like the ripping of paper. You look back to see the unsheathed pop entering her mouth.

"I purchased this delightful morsel at the church bake sale," your wife boasts, yanking the pop from her mouth with a smack. "Mrs. Dunnerrod's boys were peddling them, called the creations Cath-o-licks. 'Tis a splendidly clever marketing gimmick, no?"

Facing the copier, you roll your eyes. You swear she thinks herself a turn-of-the-century lady of leisure. Then again, all she really needs is an outrageous hat, maybe a corset or two to complete the ensemble. She has already got the itchy dresses that were, supposedly, all the rage in those days. A dignified aristocrat for a husband, a mansion upon the moors, that is the life she'd lead. In time, like all well-bred daughters, she'd yearn to travel. Her husband, who simply couldn't say no to that darling pout of hers, would graciously oblige. They'd enjoy first-class status aboard the largest luxury liner that ever did sail the seas. Wrapped tight in a Lewis's Department Store fur, she'd mosey about the ship's many decks, greeting fellow travelers and wishing them pleasant evenings, the ship a safe maiden voyage. Something would go tragically awry, however, in the early morning on April 15. Ice would hit the decks, and dear Tabitha would be asleep. 2,207 passengers would be onboard; only 712 would survive. Fiendishly, you smile. The odds would not be in her favor.

The hum of the copying machine brings you back to the present. You can feel Mrs. Kuhn's presence there, lingering behind you. You wonder why she remains in your office, why she hasn't yet left for the living room or, for

we are dna

that matter, the upstairs bathroom. Turning to face her, you tilt your head to the side.

"Is there something I can do for you, Mrs. Kuhn?"

Your words cause her to jump, to rub her eyes. Apparently you weren't the only one daydreaming. For a moment she appears disoriented but quickly regains focus. She meets your gaze.

"No," she returns, blinking away her sleepiness, "there's nothing I want of you. There is, however, something *I* can do for *you*."

She licks her lips. You're reminded of that night on the couch, that incessant banging, that mouth hanging open, agape in sexual gratification. You shake away the untimely vision.

"Well, correction," she admits, moving toward the hallway, "there's something I *did* do for you."

She swooshes out of the room only to return moments later, a business card in hand. She shoves it in your face.

AUBREY MCMILLON, SALES CONSULTANT.
DAVIS INSURANCE.

You take the card from her hand, run your fingers over the embossed lettering. Thinking that you might have missed something, you turn it over. The back is blank.

Puzzled, you give Tabitha a look.

"Is this a subtle way of telling me that you want to change our insurance provider?"

She unleashes a wicked laugh. It goes on for far too long.

"Mercy, no!" she howls, clearing her throat. "Recall for me, if you would, that oh-so-unpleasant remark that you made about church last week, how it has never exactly been—how do you say—to your benefit?"

You know what she's talking about. Your exact words were, "It doesn't do me a shittin' thing."

"Yes, well, be that as it may"—she sends a fleeting glare in your direction—"I fain believe a certain someone may soon change his proverbial tune." She crosses her arms, then waits.

You hate when she does this, when she's deliberately ambiguous, when she encourages your forcing the words from her mouth. You never want to play her game, and yet, you so seldom have a choice. Sighing, you yield to her demands, perform your role.

"Oh? And why, great enlightened one, is that?"

Just then the phone rings.

Shuffling over to your desk, you toss aside dozens of papers in an effort to unearth the caller ID.

we are dna

MCMILLON, PAUL AND AU
RESIDENTIAL: 330-966-

You hate how Tabitha demanded the purchase of a budget caller ID system, one with an LED screen that truncates names and numbers. Still, this call couldn't have come at a better time. No longer must you grovel at Tabitha's feet for information. You can just as easily get it directly from the source.

Picking up the receiver, you dismiss your wife with a flick of your wrist.

"Hello, Kuhn residence."

The voice that responds is quiet, distant, like Tabitha's that time she phoned from Europe.

"Hello," the caller breathes, her throat sounding hoarse, "is this Harold?"

You can just barely make out the words. Removing the cordless from your ear, you hold it close to your face, eyeing its dial pad for the volume button. Like a woodpecker to a tree, you hammer it several times.

"Yes, this is Harold speaking. How might I help you?"

"Hi, Harold, this is Aubrey McMillon calling. I met your wife at the St. Michael's bake sale this afternoon. She might have told you that I was going to call?" Her voice is as soft as before. The volume button, you reason, must be a placebo or, rather, the telecommunications equivalent; it makes you feel good whilst, in actuality, it does nothing.

"Yes, hi, Aubrey. Coincidentally enough, we were just talking about you."

"Oh, really? Did Tabitha tell you PSSSSSSSSH son?"

"I'm sorry, what was that?"

"Did your wife, Tab-PFFT tell you abo———son?"

"I'm sorry, dear, you're breaking up. One more time?"

"Hu———on." Silence.

You figure she's probably switching phones. Why this technology hasn't, in the course of the last fifty years or so, grown more stable you'll never understand. And now, of course, cell phones are rapidly replacing landlines as the standard means of communication. Talk about stellar audio fidelity! You've encountered so much white noise in recent years that, in all honesty, you've grown rather accustomed to its presence. No doubt about it, there's a certain comfort in those hisses, those periodic sprays of interference. Today, should you encounter crystal clear audio reception, you fear something's wrong, that the call has been dropped or, worse, tapped. You often request that your friends hang up and call you back later on when their signals are weaker. Only difficult dialogues, those marked by

we are dna

a surfeit of "whats" and "huhs," seem to put your mind at ease.

There's a click on the other end of the line. You hear shuffling, breathing, then, finally, a voice.

"HELLO? ARE YOU STILL THERE?"

Mrs. McMillon is at least ten—no, make that twenty—times louder than before. The phone is dropped from your ear and, once again, its volume button smashed. Cautiously, you reaffix it to your head.

"Yes, Aubrey, I'm here. Is everything okay on your side?"

She laughs gleefully.

"Oh, yes, I'm so sorry about that. My kids bought me one of those hands-free headsets for my birthday. So much for that."

"Yeah, I could barely hear you."

"Well, I shouldn't be surprised. That's what I get for trying to change with the times. So anyway, I'm sorry, where were we before all of that confusion?"

"We didn't get far," you say, spinning a pen in your unoccupied hand. "I believe you just told me that you met my wife at church."

"Oh, really? That's all? Damn."

Apparently she had believed the conversation further along.

"Well, anyway," she says, "we got to talking—you

brian lucas

know how we ladies do—and somehow, one way or another, we touched on the topic of your teaching piano." She pauses for a moment. "You probably know where this is going, don't you?"

"Mrs. McMillon," you purr in your caughtcha-with-your-hand-in-the-cookie-jar voice, "do you, perchance, have an interest in playing the piano?" You normally don't accept adult students, though, really, you wouldn't mind making an exception.

From the speaker comes the sound of Mrs. McMillon cackling; only it doesn't sound like a human laughing, but instead a hen clucking. Patiently you wait for her beak to close.

"Me? Me! Oh, Christ-on-a-cross, no!" You wonder if she used that phrase with Mrs. Kuhn; you doubt it, otherwise that business card would surely have "accidentally" fallen into the trash. "No, no," she denies, panting, "the only thing these hands are good for is eating!"

You want to ask her if she has ever heard of a fork or a knife. You think better of it.

"Actually, Mr. Kuhn, I was thinking about my son, Andrew. That boy has got music in his veins. He was involved in some piano recitals in elementary school, nothing too elaborate, but I'll tell you what, he showed promise. He kept up with his training in middle school. There was a coach in-house who showed him a thing or two, got him

we are dna

real comfortable with the whole two-handed form. I thought the guy a real maestro, but I dunno, something about him rubbed Andy the wrong way, I guess. Last month, when classes resumed, he told me he'd like to continue with piano but only if I'd get him a real teacher, one outside of the public school system, you know?"

"I understand," you say. "Some students learn better outside of the classroom."

"Yeah. I, uh, I feel kinda bad, though, because I sort of dropped the ball on this one. I didn't really make an earnest effort in seeking out another tutor. To be honest, I forgot all about this whole predicament until this afternoon when I was chatting with your wife. She told me you teach piano, and goddamn, it was like a frickin' lightbulb went on in my head. I dunno, talk about good timing! Hell, maybe this is God's way of repaying my good behavior during that priest's lame-ass sermons."

You don't really know how to respond to that, whether or not you should laugh or gasp. You decide to pretend that you didn't hear it.

"Have you talked this all over with your son, Mrs. McMillon?" you ask, genuinely concerned. "I don't know if my wife told you, but I've made it a policy to refuse instruction to unwilling students."

"Unwilling? ... Oh, right, you're talking about demanding parents, huh? Nothing to worry about here. My

God, I could give a shit less if Andrew plays or doesn't play. Don't worry, Mr. Kuhn; this hunger for music is entirely his. Hey, you wanna talk to him? He's right here."

"Oh, no, really. Mrs. McMillon, it's fine. I trust your word." You realize that your talking is of no use. She has already pulled the phone from her ear, is covering its mouthpiece with her thumb, is hollering for her son's attention. You think it funny how the universal language among families seems to be the scream.

"Hey, Andrew! ANDREW! ... Nate, where's my son? ... Can you tell him to come down here, please? Tell him he has a phone call. ... No, I want him to use the one down here. ... Because I said so, that's why!"

You seriously contemplate hanging up the phone, think about freeing Andrew from what you believe an inopportune interview. No teenager in his or her right mind would want to spend even five minutes of a Sunday night blabbing with an adult—a teacher, no less. Sad to say, you're already beginning to despise Mrs. McMillon; she reminds you too much of Tabitha, casts you deep into uncertain waters, demands that you swim. Few moments in life are more unpleasant, more uncomfortable than those during which you're forced to do something that you detest and, worse, to do it with flair. In times like these, the best you can muster is a wobbly smile. It teeters, it totters, and before too long, it falls apart.

we are dna

You detect motion on the other end of the line. The cordless is changing hands. Another pair of lungs is breathing, exhaling louder and deeper than before.

"This is Andrew." His voice reminds you of molasses, dark and thick. It catches you as unusually baritone, especially for a pubescent teenager.

"Hey, Andrew. Your mom tells me you like to play the piano."

The boy says nothing, but you can hear him breathing. You worry that perhaps your signal faded, that your greeting was improperly relayed.

"Did you hear me?"

"Dude," moans the Tom Jones wannabe, "who is this?"

Before you can answer, you hear Mrs. McMillon braying in the background.

"Don't be a jackass, Andy! It's that piano teacher I was telling you about, Harold Kuhn." She starts to speak in a whisper. "Be sure to call him 'mister.'"

"Oh, yeah, yeah, yeah, I'm sorry about that!"

You can't tell to whom the boy is apologizing, to you or his mother. On the fence, you think it best to wait quietly.

"No, I didn't mean any disrespect, sir"—now you know that he's talking to you—"it's just that my friends often harass me about my playing the piano. They think anything that's artistic is gay."

"Well, have you given 'em a piece of your mind?"

"You bet. Every time they get on my back, they hear about it. They're starting to cool it down, though."

"Well, good. Don't let anyone denigrate your music. That's a significant part of who you are." You're concerned the words came off a bit strained. You genuinely meant them. "I'm serious," you add for good measure.

"Yeah, that's what I've been telling them. It'll sink in one of these days."

"So what do you think about taking some lessons? Are you up to the challenge?" You want to stir up some fire in the kid's soul, get him passionate about his craft.

"Hell, yeah!" he hollers.

"ANDREW!" Mrs. McMillon screams from afar. "LANGUAGE!"

"I meant 'heck, yeah.'" You can tell that he's making a deliberate effort to sound as dispassionate as possible, to further fan his mother's frustration.

"All right," you say, opening your organizer to the upcoming week, "when would you like to start?"

"How about tomorrow?"

You're taken aback by the ferocity of his enthusiasm. He honestly can't seem to wait.

"Hm, let's see." You consult the planner in front of you. "I have a three o'clock open. What time do you finish

we are dna

school?"

"Two." You hear the familiar sound of a thumb upon the mouthpiece. "Hey, Mom, can you drive me to Mr. Kuhn's for a lesson tomorrow at three? ... You can? Do you know how to get there? ... Okay, I'll tell him." The thumb is removed. "That should work out just fine, Mr. Kuhn. My mom says that your wife gave her your home address. We can just GPS it."

"Andrew," you hear Mrs. McMillon beckon, "is Nate staying over for dinner?" You hear the *cling-cling-cling* of a metal spoon against the side of a pot.

"Yeah, and overnight too, if that's all right."

"Tonight's a school night," the concerned parent reminds.

"Well, we do go to the same school, you know." Andrew laughs. "I've already done my homework."

"Fine. Tell Mr. Kuhn we'll see him at three."

Andrew guffaws into the phone.

"Did you hear that? We'll see you at three."

"All right, I look forward to it, Andrew. Tell your mom that my lessons are forty-five minutes to an hour long. She's welcome to either wait in our living room or go where she pleases. You'll be done at four."

{

brian lucas

Sleep doesn't come easily that night, not for you or Mrs. Kuhn. While she complains of hard pillows, too soft a mattress, you feel not unlike a kindergartener on Christmas Eve. Something glorious is going to happen tomorrow, you just know it, and nothing and nobody, certainly not the sandman, is going to stand in your way. Yes, indeed, jubilance is most definitely imminent. Though your rational mind tells you to calm down, that your anticipation is unfounded, your adrenal glands say otherwise. Your heart has been instructed to thump its way out of your chest, your brain to buzz to the brink of destruction. Blood is pumping through your veins at what's surely a perilous speed. Despite the fact that tomorrow's schedule is as unremarkable as can be (white tea, two lessons, C-SPAN), you feel yourself on a precipice, about to embark on a mighty plunge. To hell with logic and proportion, restraint and reserve; you haven't felt this good in years.

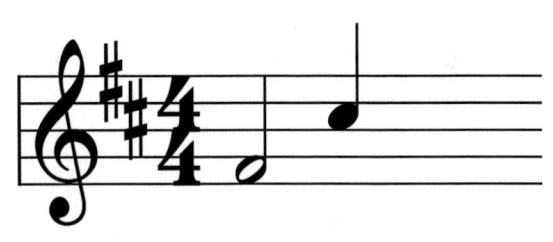

The next morning never comes—not to your conscious mind, anyway. Monday afternoon, 12:55 PM. Your soul stirs to the melodic chirp of a songbird, eyes open to the caress of a gentle breeze. The bedroom windows are open, their full-length curtains billowing in the wind. Beyond the semi-sheer voiles lies a sky of blue, not a single cloud, not even a puff of fluff, in sight. From the acreage around you comes the sound of a chainsaw buzzing, a lawnmower coughing to a start. You listen as a neighborhood girl unleashes a blood-curdling scream, is told that she's "it" and must count to twenty. All around you whirl signs and sensations of life, indications of humanity at work and play. Yet alone in your bedroom you lie, a misplaced cog in the machinery of society.

Tossing your arm over the right side of the bed, you

fondle blindly for your watch. From the moment you locate it and survey its screen, your day goes downhill. You slept in late, *really* late. In just over an hour's time, Rachelle Mew, your most inscrutable student, will be ringing the doorbell. Your wife will hear it on its first ring—she always does—and seeing as she spends her Mondays gentrifying your office (her word, not yours), she should be able to answer the door within seconds. She'll choose to wait five minutes.

Rachelle has been a student of yours for three years now. She has never, not even once, canceled or rescheduled an appointment. "If I commit myself to an engagement," she once told you, "I make it my business to be present." Sustaining this impeccable attendance record has not been without difficulty, without sacrifice on her part. She reminds you of this often. "Oh, yeah," she confides, tossing her head back as if it were a beer, "I mean I've missed birthdays, funerals, family functions, you name it." She prides herself on the absoluteness of her dedication. It disturbs you.

Your shower that afternoon is an entirely utilitarian affair. There's no soulful singing, no slow caress of your body, no meticulous shampooing of your hair. A loofa over your chest and crotch, a dime of gel to your scalp, and you're outta there. Blotting down your body with a towel, you scurry to your closet and grab a generic polo and pant.

we are dna

You dress while making the bed. Fluff a pillow, throw on your shirt. Spread the sheet, button your collar. Pile on the comforter, hoist up your slacks.

Returning to the bathroom, you feed the sink your tea. It gulps it down slowly, painfully. You know the feeling. You brush your teeth for a count of ten seconds. You floss for six. The gingivitis doesn't even have time to die.

As you make for the stairs, your bowels begin to growl. Better check the watch. 1:48 PM. *Sorry, body, there's no time for that.* You feel the squeeze in every sense of the word. Hoping that the sensation will pass, that the desire will dissipate, you begin your descent. By the time you reach the bottom rung, you detect motion. Your bowels are on the move. *Shit!* Literally.

Rachelle Mew ding-dongs her way into the house at 1:58 PM. You are otherwise engaged in the downstairs bathroom until 2:06 PM. You arrive in your study at 2:08 and apologize for the delay. Rachelle, outfitted in a violet jumper, is talking at Tabitha. Your wife, being her usual pleasant self, is paying no attention and, with her back turned, has begun dusting a bookcase. Upon your entrance, she stops.

"What took you so long?" she jaws, shaking out her dusting wand. "That Moo girl has been here for a quarter hour."

You love how your wife never regulates her expressions, never censors her speech. Rachelle Mew is right there, present, in your office and has introduced herself to your wife upwards of seven times. Rachelle, though peculiar in the extreme, is a polite girl. To her, Tabitha has always been "Mrs. Kuhn." Your wife, on the other hand, cares little for small talk and even less for propriety. She's in your study for one purpose and one purpose alone—to clean. Even if rightly baited, if asked a question, Tabitha won't bite. Rachelle, quite simply, isn't worth her time. And learning the girl's name? Ha! That's definitely not worth the effort. After all, why struggle when "that Moo girl" will do just fine? Sure, it may not get the job done *nicely* but, hell, it gets it done, doesn't it? In Tabitha's mind that's good enough.

Rachelle looks especially unkempt, disheveled today. In all of the years that you've spent with her, you've never gotten to the bottom of that hair, never figured out why it flops, why it frizzes the way it does. There's one thing you know for certain: it's not people hair. No, it has got to be synthetic. Human hair doesn't grow like that in long, sweeping tendrils, doesn't form like that in loosely wound ropes not unlike yarn, and most certainly doesn't tint like that into a puslike mustard. But still, above all of this, disregarding its ribbon-like structure, wooly design, and insufferable color, Rachelle's hair is, peculiarly enough, completely and utterly lusterless. There is not a single ounce of

we are dna

polish, not a mere molecule of oil throughout the whole of her mane—at least, not in the thirty-odd inches of it that you've seen. What happens to the rest—what it looks like, how it's restrained—you'll never know. Wherever she goes, whatever she wears, Rachelle bulges in the rear and not from ass, oh, no, but hair.

Today's grape jumper comes as a surprise, as she's seldom seen in anything else but discount outlet blue jeans—the ones with the rubberized elastic waist, good for the store and keeping of hair. Into the pants goes anything and everything that drapes below the small of her back, be it shirt, hair, or the occasional woodland burr, for that matter. You reason she must especially fancy this jumper, seeing as it lacks the necessary hair compartment and, as a result, required special alteration, special effort on her part. You admire her workmanship; she handled the tailoring nicely. Just above the jumper's rear pockets is a slim horizontal hem into which the yellow curtain has been smoothed. Despite its being only inches away from the opening of the garment's shorts, this makeshift hairway somehow inhibits the locks from reemerging around the girl's thighs. You chuckle to yourself, envisioning the elaborate hair rerouting system which must be in place so as to prevent such an overflow.

Rachelle's lesson goes well, if not exceedingly so. Though she fumbles a few notes, she recovers well and on a second play-through makes a flawless execution. You hate to admit it, but the girl has really got talent. She's one of your few students who, when performing a piece, seems to have evolved beyond nervousness, beyond fear of blunder. It's a pivotal moment in a pianist's life, the moment when one stops fighting the piano, stops fighting with his or her ego, and achieves, for the very first time, a harmonious accord between body and mind, instrument and musician. To be sure, it's something to, if not celebrate, then at the very least acknowledge.

Meek as a twenty-something poli-sci major is jaded, Rachelle receives your praise with quiet appreciation, a reddening of the cheeks. Her hair frays in jubilance. You gift unto her a recently purchased piano song book, *Bittersweet Lovesongs,* and instruct her to select a piece of her choice for next week's performance. She shouldn't make too elaborate of preparations; you'll work on it together. As she goes to leave, she mouths something (perhaps "Thank you"?) before shuffling to the door and out into the hall. On the groove in the bench's cushion where her buttocks sat is a check for thirty dollars. Written on the document's memo line are the words "For Lesson #141." You find that just a wee bit odd.

Andrew is not what you expected, in the best possible way. On the telephone he sounded like an eighteen-year-old asshole, a self-professed "dude who bangs bitches," a queen bee among his soon-to-be-frat-boy buddies. Now, granted, you don't know of many jocks who take an active interest in piano, but still you had your doubts. It doesn't help that his physical appearance matches your expectations almost perfectly.

Mrs. Kuhn escorts him into your office. She seldom does that, only when she expects your students to be vandals or petty thieves, if not in this lifetime, then surely the last. You hear the doorknob turn and look back expectantly. A young man, probably a recent high school graduate, stands in the frame and quickly surveys his surroundings. Amber-skinned and physically sculpted, he's of an

brian lucas

athletic build and medium height, with dark features and a smile too bright to be natural. His hair is careless yet manicured, his ears pierced and studded (cubic zirconia, no doubt), his shirt tight and sleeveless. Definitely the "I waste hos" type. Seeming hesitant to enter, he withdraws, flashing Tabitha a sideways grin.

"After you."

She's unimpressed. *Who do you think you're fooling*, her eyes seem to criticize. She struts forward with her head at a bizarre angle, careful to keep him in her peripheral. He seemed a little bit too intrigued with that gallery reproduction of the *Venus of Urbino*. She'll be sure to check for it before duly seeing him out.

"Mr. Kuhn, this is Mr. McMitchon, your three o'clock."

With that she turns and withdraws, slamming the door on the way.

The muscle-bound stud saunters to the center of the room, where he stands awkwardly. He seems strangely uneasy, especially for a guy who likely enjoys more than his share of sexual encounters—if not consummated then at least proposed ones. Nothing inflates an ego, you've come to learn, like good looks. Then again, maybe not. Andrew seems a curious exception to that rule. You stand up, ready a premade formal greeting.

"Hi, Mr. McMillon, it's a pleasure to meet you." You

we are dna

take his hand, shake it vigorously. His grasp is firm but, to your delight, not oppressively so. His skin is silky, luxurious. "Gorgeous day we're having, isn't it?"

"Yeah, me and my buddies kill for this weather," he says with another sideways smile. "And please, call me Andrew. No. Actually, call me Andy."

He smells like a spicy peppermint. The cologne is potent, maybe on the verge of being overpowering. You wonder why Mrs. Kuhn didn't fall to the floor in spasms, didn't begin speaking in tongues.

"Well, whoever you are," you say, trying to keep matters light, "nice to meet you. Please take a seat." You motion to a leather club chair near the window, in front of that hideous ficus Mrs. Kuhn refuses to move elsewhere. Even though its leaves are plastic, they appear to be wilting. You make a mental note to trash it on garbage day.

In taking his seat, the jock's sport shorts begin a slow and steady ascension up his thighs. The skin there, unsurprisingly, is also olive. He wriggles his hips as the seat engulfs his frame. The shorts are now wholly and completely heaped about his crotch. It's only a matter of time before his manhood makes an appearance, rolls out onto the leather. You want to say something, advise his adjusting the article, moving to another seat, one less—say—accommodating, but can't think of a way to broach the subject without seeming vulgar, indecent, or, worse, anticipatory. He rests his hands on his pecs. You decide he's either oblivious, an exhibitionist, or both. Afraid that your gaze might naturally drift downward, that although you have no desire to see his flesh, you can't help but look, you initiate a conversation.

"So how old are you, Andrew? Oh, God, where are my manners?! Can I get you a drink or something to eat? We have water, Diet Coke, tea … well, white tea, um … what else …"

"No, no, I'm cool," he asserts, sliding his hands downward, feeling his abs through his shirt. "I'm fifteen."

It's impossible.

"I'm sorry, how old are you?" You release an awkward chuckle. "I thought I just heard you say you're fifteen."

His eyes narrow. He looks somewhat insulted.

"That's right," he says. "I am."

You do everything within your power to conceal your shock.

"Oh, okay." Awkward silence. "Forgive me, Andrew—"

"Andy."

"Right, Andy, but I pegged you for an eighteen-year-old, maybe even nineteen."

He pushes out his lower lip, nods slowly.

"No, it's cool, happens a lot, actually. I went through puberty when I was like ten."

we are dna

You're surprised by how comfortable he is talking about puberty, describing its onset. Most of the younger teenagers that you've met prefer to pretend that it isn't happening, to ignore the blatant reality.

"When do you turn sixteen?" you ask, hoping that it's soon.

You're not exactly fond of the severe level of parental involvement experienced when students are without wheels of their own. It's fine if the parents act as chauffeurs, dropping their students off at the door, picking them up in the same way. What's unfortunate is that most parents are not unlike Brandine's—overly involved in their children's lives, overly obsessed with appearing both "cool" and dedicated. Despite every indication, they fail to realize that the best kind of parent, in their kids' eyes as well as in those of their mentors, is a largely aloof, relatively distant one. It's one thing to be supportive; it's another thing to be intrusive, invasive. Few can see the difference.

"In January," Andy responds, "January fifth." He appears excited at this prospect. "I've already got my temps, got 'em in early June. Mom has taken me around town a few times. Next is the highway."

"Very cool," you reply. "So what do you say you show me what you can do on the piano?"

"Ready and willing!" the boy in a man's body pronounces. With palms down on the arms of the chair, he

brian lucas

pulls himself vertical by way of a tricep flex. There's movement in his athletic shorts. For a split-second you think you see something. A patch of swarthy skin. A bulging vein. Then nothing. Nylon mesh. You feel a tinge of guilt for seizing this opportunity, for beholding a forbidden sight, for gazing upon an unripened fruit, but most of all, for desperately seeking what you care not to see. Supposedly.

〜

Andrew McMillon, as you come to find out, is not only a superbly talented pianist but also a ferociously impassioned one, a tooth-banger as they are called in the industry. Caught up in the moment, in his ardor for the art, he doesn't so much play the keys as he pounds them, slamming them down as if they were whack-a-moles or objects of loathing. It's something that you will have to work on, the tempering of his passion or, if not that, then at least the intensity of its outward expression. Though fine in some arenas, some venues, tooth-banging is not universally well-loved. In short, it's not unlike a pair of hot pants in the entertainment world—something many spurn, many downright avoid, and only a few can successfully pull off. It can be used to one's advantage but always and only if the situation warrants. A general rule of thumb: Don't tooth-

we are dna

bang at dinner parties.

To demonstrate his musical competence, Andy performs two pieces—"Whitewashed Days, Torrid Nights" and "The Choleric Ransomer." They are highly involved, ambitious pieces, all the more so for a person of his age, his youth. Playing from memory, the music stand sitting empty, vacant, his execution is remarkably fluid. Unlike most amateur pianists, he keeps ahead of the music, is always anticipating the next string of notes, the next rise or fall. He leads rather than follows the music, is the engine steaming ahead not the caboose teetering behind. As his performance draws to a close, you grow increasingly agog and simply cannot wait to show him what is next, how to leave the rails and earn his wings. There are truly no words to describe just how alive, how vital you feel in the company of a like-minded individual, someone who shares your fanaticism, your fervor for soulful expression. Someone like Andy. Allowing his inner experimentalist to shine, he improvises his finale, concluding first with a crescendo then a slap of a bass note. He looks to you expectantly, eager for critique. Though he's a mere acquaintance, just fifteen minutes less of a stranger, you feel an energy, a magnetism which cannot be denied. One of you is a celestial body, the other its satellite. You don't know which is which, but, frankly, you don't care. The configuration is not the important thing here. What is important, however,

brian lucas

what's damn near necessary is that Andrew becomes a perennial student of yours, that this bond prospers, thrives. Compatible souls are a most rare and special find. They mustn't be squandered but nurtured, cultivated, encouraged to reach their maximum potential.

You know this is the beginning of a beautiful thing. You won't be letting it go.

Andrew visits on Mondays and Fridays. They've easily become your favorite days of the week. Excepting Rachelle, he's your most punctual student—or his mother is, rather. Ten 'til three, twice a week, a red sedan in your tulip bed. Thankfully it's autumn and not spring. Mrs. Kuhn has yet to notice. She's too busy bagging bushes in the backyard, trying to protect her most cherished shrubs from that which is inevitable—frostbite. The nights are growing cooler, the days shorter. You look at the calendar. October 23. The weeks pass by too quickly. According to that blonde skank on the Weather Channel, we're to expect snow before Halloween. Busting out of her top as she gesticulates about the green screen, she accidentally drops her pen remote, the one with which she advances the slides. Bumbling something about a sexy front going southward, she squats down and, in reaching forward, spreads her legs. She shows the world her world. You never see her on TV again.

Rachelle has just departed, her two o'clock lesson complete. Her check was not under her ass this time but discreetly placed in the wicker basket out of which springs the ficus. She has apparently confused Halloween with Easter. You never much liked egg hunts. You despise nest egg hunts all the more. Retrieving the check, you walk it over to your desk. Thirty dollars paid to the order of Mr. Harold Kuhn. "Lesson #148." You chuckle to yourself, a shallow, half-hearted, I'm-a-bad-person chuckle.

The reality is Rachelle hasn't received a worthwhile lesson in weeks. Not since Lesson #141. To call the seven that followed half-baked would be a gross understatement. Anxious to once again encounter Andy, to inhale that tangy peppermint, to hear his soul transformed into song, you misspend your Mondays and Fridays in mindless stupor. Your preoccupation is stubborn, your treatment of Rachelle deplorable.

Every week she's greeted by a limp handshake. As she flits over to the piano, her ream of yarn bounces out a hello. You pretend not to notice. She sits down, fingers her songbook, locates a piece, and begins to play. As the instrument's brought to life, you stand behind her, pacing. After so many years of experience, your ears have become

we are dna

accustomed to hearing mistakes, hiccups, miscalculated moves. She makes many of each. Your noticing this is not conscious but subconscious, kind of like one's knowing whether a traffic light is red or green. It doesn't impact your stream of consciousness. You continue to obsess and fantasize, to hypothesize about what Andy might do or say, how he might look, what he might wear. Rachelle finishes the piece and, for a moment, beams quietly. Playing piano means as much to her as it does to Andy, probably more. She not only garners immense joy from the extracurricular but also a profound sense of satisfaction. She believes it her true calling, the reason for her existence on this Earth, the gift she must sharpen, then share with the world. In your catatonia you don't know this. Due to your apathy you won't know this. It will remain her little secret, one which she tried to communicate but which was lost in translation.

In time, her euphoria, the result of a job well done, abates. She turns around, peeps at you from her lowly position upon the bench. Wholly unmoved, you continue to pace back and forth, head nodding slowly. It's as if she never stopped playing, as if her selection never came to an end. She knows you as an attentive instructor. Surely you were listening, analyzing, assessing. Surely you heard her struggle with that second diminution. Surely you found her finale impeccable, well-paced, poignant. Maybe you're just deep in thought, struggling to find the words with which to express your criticism. She waits a few more seconds. No change. She dismisses her theory and adopts another—that her teacher is losing touch with reality, suffering from some insidious disease.

She's probably right. You're not well. You like to believe you are, sure, but deep inside, below the many facades, the many fabrications, the many illusory notions, you know something has gone awry. Four weeks ago you were an entirely different man—a composed, dignified, and reasonably well-adjusted retiree who, in entering the autumn of his life, has accepted the body's eventual decline with poise, grace, and quiet resignation. Since Monday, September 28, the day of the slowly receding sport shorts, nothing has been the same. You can't feign ignorance, pretend the source of this shift unknown. "I dunno" won't suffice, not by a long shot. You know the catalyst of this change all too well. He smells like a breath mint.

In front of a mirror you've practiced saying the words, divulging your feelings. It is of no use; again and again the sentiment sounds contrived. And really, why shouldn't it? You've known the boy for less than a month. Three and a half weeks of quivering hands and quaking knees does not a true love make. Infatuation, maybe, but surely not love. An emotion such as this takes months to form, spends years in leavening. You can't make ciabatta in a day; you

we are dna

can't stir love in twenty-five. You can't, and yet, bending the laws of attraction, you have.

Pulling back the curtains, you take another glance out the window. No car in the flowerbed, no turf marks on the lawn. You clutch your right wrist, feel for your watch. There's no Swiss contraption to be found, just dry skin and lumpy veins. You forgot your watch upstairs. You've been forgetting a lot of things lately. Two days in a row now you've forgotten to "drink" your white tea. Tabitha has noticed. The glass disappears midday, is presumably washed, then reappears the next morning. She has yet to confront you on the matter. One more slip-up and you can expect a note. You glance about the room, eye the cuckoo clock on the wall. 2:45 PM. Rachelle chose to end her lesson early. Supposedly she was "running late for an appointment." You knew it was a lie the moment it trickled out of her mouth. Rachelle never double-books. Surely next will come a missed lesson. Then two. Then an excuse as to why she must discontinue instruction, an awkward good-bye.

A wintry draft passes through your office. You shiver. It's almost time to fire up the radiator, ushering in yet another five months of clanking pipes and steaming vents. You look forward to the day the house explodes, a conflagration of smoke and asbestos darkening the sky. Gone would be the boastful staircase, bitter tea, that loveless bed. All would be renewal—well, either that or death.

You hear the crunch of mulch under over-inflated tires. The sedan doesn't even stop. Forward propulsion enduring, the passenger door opens, and out trips Andy. Mommy McMillon accelerates, and as the car bounces down off the curb, Andy's door, still ajar, whips shut. An amicable double honk and she's off. Head down, the forsaken teen starts his trek up the sidewalk, watching his feet clap the pavement. Crossing paths with Tabitha's spooktacular Halloween display, he stops to study its many poorly crafted props.

This year's exhibit is what Mrs. Kuhn calls a "ghoul-infested faux cemetery, the most excellent yard installation of the whole witching season." In reality, it is little more than a few cardboard cutouts which have been spray-painted gray and adorned with trite inscriptions by way of permanent marker. They alternate between "R.I.P." and "Love Thy Afterlife." Tabitha believes the tombstones ingenious, their engravings "witty and wise." Beside these masterful creations sit two slowly shrinking blocks of hay. The blustery October winds have not been kind to either of the buy-one-get-one-free bales. A fine layer of displaced straw and hay now rests atop the grass, the yard thus appearing recently reseeded. The drab display was topped off with a scattering of gourds ranging in size from organic to steroid-injected. Tabitha believed their inclusion

we are dna

"integral," seeing as they "unified the polarized components of the composition, tied the autumnal to the occult." The lot of them have since been relocated to the street where, under the auspices of night, each was smashed. A pulpy residue remains where the hose couldn't reach.

Unimpressed, Andy walks on, his pecs tightening with the sweep of his feet. Scratching his head, he squints into the sun then, lowering his eyes, takes in the exterior of your house. He seems to be scanning the windows, one at a time, starting with those of the second floor. When his gaze meets the panes of your office, he seems initially intrigued, then decidedly unnerved. Mid-gait he freezes. His eyes lock on to you. He doesn't blink, doesn't smile, doesn't wave. Just stares. You think that you detect a tightening of his eyebrows, a furrowing of his brow, the formation of a glare, perhaps. Your vision beginning to blur, you have little choice but to blink. Your eyelids drop, then retract, a strobe of black, then clarity, color, and ... motion? Yes, motion. Someone, something has just streaked across your lawn, whisked by at a frenetic speed. You eye Tabitha's horrible horrorfest. Andy is no longer in sight, no longer glowering at you but is gone, absent, missing in action. There's a clanking, bonging, a gonging in the hallway. The doorbell is ringing.

Warily, you trip the deadbolt, peek out the eyehole. No murderer or monster is in sight, no obstruction—be it finger, thumb, or palm—deliberately blocking your view. You pull open the pair of mahogany artifacts which, in the winter of their lives, serve as your house's front doors (they too were extracted from a Parisian theatre). There on your front porch stands Andy, his right arm flexed, holding his left at the elbow. He smiles warmly and winks.

"How are ya, Mr. K? Another beautiful day we're having, huh?" He shifts his weight from his left to his right foot. He is wearing running shoes, filthy ones at that. You assume they were once white; their tongues still appear so. The rest of them, however—their tops, sides, backs, and laces—is mud-drenched. This sneaker soil is not old, not dry, cracked, and flaking but rather new, recent, gooey. It shines in the sunlight.

"Hey, Andrew," you greet, your tone flat. You drop your eyes. "Uh, what happened down there?"

For an instant Andy appears baffled. He looks down, then, in realizing the issue, chuckles.

"Oh, you mean *that*?" Kicking back his right foot, he rotates his ankle as if to remind himself of the severity of the stain. "Wow," he announces, "I sure did a nice job gumming these up." He turns his attention to his left foot. "My friends and I were practicing lacrosse after school today; nothing too serious, just tossing the ball back and forth—you know—trying out some defensive maneuvers." The left ankle begins its spin cycle, thrashing about more

we are dna

wildly than had the right. "I, uh, guess we kicked up a little more mud than was expected." He raises his eyes but not his head; he purses his lips. He's blushing. "Should I take them off?"

"I think that'd be a good idea." You crane your neck to the left, to the right, in search of Tabitha. No wife, just grass and straw. She mustn't be done yet with her backyard bush-bagging. "Maybe Mrs. Kuhn can spray 'em down with the hose before you go," you offer, watching as he struggles to remove the shoes without dirtying his socks.

"Nah, it's cool," he says. "There'll be a lot more where that came from." He deftly slips his feet out of the shoes and shoves the juicy high-tops aside. There they deflate, cave in on themselves like rain-soaked moccasins. Realizing that your body is blocking the doorway, you step aside, permitting the boy's entrance. The polished hardwood like ice, he glides inside. You almost don't notice the manly way in which his calf muscles tighten, the lusty manner in which his ass squeezes and releases. You tell yourself to think ordinary thoughts, to put your mind elsewhere.

"Let's stop by the kitchen and grab something to drink before we get started," you suggest, tilting your head to the side. The boy nods bashfully. Escorting your student down the corridor, you keep your eyes on the floor, watching its many planks disappear under your feet. The wood is a Brazilian cherry. Its cuts are stiff and long.

{

You shove a glass into the device on the refrigerator's door. You wait as the water is dispensed in a steady stream. You ask Andy if he's thirsty. He thanks you for the offer but declines. You stand together in the otherwise vacant room. The lights are off; a gentle hum is emanating from the automatic dishwasher. An indicator light notifies you that it is sanitizing. You tell yourself to do the same, to dispel the perversion from your mind, to disinfect your otherwise dirty thoughts, your dubious intentions. The boy is tracing a figure eight on the marble island. He looks up at you. His lips are wet.

"Where's Mrs. Kuhn? I was expecting her to answer the door."

You swallow down one last gulp, drop the glass into the sink. It clinks but doesn't break.

"That's a good question, Andy. Where is Mrs. Kuhn?" You stroll over to the sliding glass doors, the ones that open out onto your back porch. You put your nose against the plate glass. Andy follows suit. The two of you watch as Tabitha flitters about the backyard, a pair of yellow-handled pruning shears stuffed in her back pocket. Her curveless frame is clad in a polyethylene rain poncho,

we are dna

the type sold at amusement parks and stadiums on stormy days. The hood is up. There's not a cloud for miles.

Unblinking, Andy begins to speak.

"What's she wearing? It looks like a tent made out of cellophane." Personally you think it bears more resemblance to an oversized sandwich bag, but you keep this to yourself.

"Have you ever heard of Angel Falls?"

Andy's expression is blank; his eyes are empty. It's his way of saying, "I don't want to look dumb, but I have no idea what you're talking about." He pops a finger in his mouth and throws it back deep, begins scraping at a molar.

"Angel Falls is a long-tumbling, free-falling waterfall," you lecture, watching the boy-dentist at work, "one of the world's longest, in fact."

Despite the finger lodged in his mouth, Andy tries to talk.

"Lak Niaga Talls?" He continues rooting about his oral cavity. Your brain struggles to decipher the garbled words. Eventually you get it: *Like Niagara Falls?*

"Not quite," you say, hoping that you understood him correctly. "They're located in a South American country, I know that. Oh, now which one is it? …" You scratch your head. "If my mind serves me correctly, I think it's Venezuela, but eh, that's not the important thing. What matters is that Tabith—er, I mean, Mrs. Kuhn traveled there several years ago with her father. They went to see the falls on a very warm but very rainy day. Mrs. Kuhn lacked forethought back in those days and, as a result, forgot to pack rainwear. That poncho you see her in today is the very same one which was purchased back in Venezuela on her way to the falls. I guess she sees it as a kind of souvenir. In Venezuela it kept off the rain, and here it keeps off the wind ... or at least so she tells me." You shrug, knowing your answer far more involved than Andy had anticipated. You decide to remain quiet until called upon.

In hard but not uncomfortable silence the two of you stand, quietly observing your wife's horticultural endeavors. She is kneeling down in a bed close to that dreary patch of woods, the one which flanks your property. Her hands are busy, the pruning shears gone from her pocket. Though her torso is blocking your view, you can surmise, from her body language, what she's likely doing. Her shoulders are scrunched, and her back is bent; her hands are presumably meeting right around her knees. Her forearms are at ninety-degree angles with her upper arms, her elbows pulling away from her body then drawing in close. You reason she must be pumping the shears, excising something dead or ugly from the mulch.

All of sudden the pumping stops. You watch as the shears are thrown to the ground, one of the blades stabbing the earth. Slowly, as if in shock, your wife tips backward,

we are dna

falls on her rear. The poncho breaks her fall, protects her from the grass. Before her lies a toppled pricker bush, its base branch amputated from the root. The pierced bark is birch in color. It didn't survive the season.

With a gloved hand, Tabitha lifts the thorny carcass from the ground. After holding it at chest level, she brings it to her face. Her lips touch one of its many twigs. Pushing with her thumb, she rotates the spiky mass. Her lips impress themselves upon another twig. The process repeats. Yet another twig touches her mouth. Then another. Still another. She opens her mouth, draws forth her tongue. She tries, in vain, to titillate the shrub. You wish that you hadn't required a drink, that you and Andy had proceeded directly to your study. You don't know how to explain this, but more than that, you don't even want to try.

Andy looks at you, distressed.

"Mr. Kuhn, what is she doing? Is she ... making out with that plant?"

You reach behind the boy, clutch a string, and give it a sharp tug to the right. The blinds crash downward. You spin a white rod. The blinds flap against one another, closing tightly. Dropping a hand on the boy's shoulder, you draw him out of the kitchen and into your office. What you had wanted to see was a gardener tending to her plants—no more, no less. Instead, what you got was a fleeting glimpse into the seedy underworld of girl-on-plant action. Just like when you caught your wife crouched down on the floor in the upstairs bathroom, her body oozing sex, this is another sight of which you'll never again speak.

ξ

Andrew's lesson doesn't go well today, which, for you, is a very, very good thing. The piece that you've assigned him is insanely hard, one which you yourself, up until last year, could barely even play. You can tell that he's making an earnest attempt, that he's doing everything in his power to conquer the notes, to tame the unruly tune. You smile deviously. With his every wrong note, your pulse quickens, your hands tremble with excitement. He's failing miserably and yet oh so perfectly. You love him in his shortcomings.

You allow him three do-overs. They do no good. Each performance is pithy, under thirty seconds in length. The fingerings are peculiar, erratic, the composition unforgiving. One missed note and you're done for. There's no way to recuperate, to recover. The song speeds ahead, and you're left woefully behind.

The boy is visibly irked. Feeling defeated, he drops his head, rests it on the keyboard. As his shirt rides up his back, a strip of olive skin is exposed. The muscles beneath are toned; the flesh stretched over them appears supple, firm. He wears his jeans low, dangerously low. From your

we are dna

vantage point, you know his underwear of choice to be briefs—tight, close-fitting briefs—the preferred choice of strippers and escorts worldwide. The underwear is supported by a black elastic band which, to your displeasure, rests just above Andrew's buttocks. The briefs themselves are an electric red.

In your mind's eye, you envision their being taken off, tossed carelessly onto one of the ficus's many branches. Andrew would be shirtless, would be pantless, his whole world on display. Never before would anyone else have had the pleasure of seeing it in its present form—a pubescent temple—save perhaps the boy's pediatrician. It would be a Harold Kuhn exclusive to observe the boy's budding manhood, to inspect his hills and hollows, to trace the contours of his body not with a gloved hand or metal instrument but a spongy finger pad, a velvety palm.

You're not gay. At least you don't think you are. No—Jesus Christ—you can't be. For fifty-seven years (this year, for obvious reasons, doesn't count) you've thought of nothing but women, touching women, pleasing women. In your teens you had fooled around with several. You've since made love to three. So what if you've been celibate for a fifth of your life, haven't been with a woman, with Tabitha, in years? That's irrelevant, a moot point; it has no real bearing on your sexuality. What about your recent purchase of several gay and bisexual adult films? Those were nothing more than impulse buys desired for no reason other than their shock value. They were a way to get back at Tabitha, remember? A nonaggressive means by which to exact revenge. It's not as if you ran home, clawed apart the shrink-wrap, and watched them to your heart's—and libido's—content ... well, okay, so what if that did happen? It was only once. Your hormones were not so much raging because of the man-love but rather because of the scandal of it all, the illicitness of the act. In a way, it was a form of infidelity, you know? Emotional, mental infidelity. Tell me that doesn't get a heart racing, a mind frantic. So why exactly is Andrew naked in your fantasies? You've yet to devise a reason, an excuse for that. You'll find one soon enough. You just might have to get a little creative, that's all. There is a way to spin any story, any reality, as long as you have the will. And you do. You're intent upon keeping yourself in denial for as long as possible. If you keep telling yourself that it's not there, maybe, just maybe, it will fall away.

You vow to work on deluding yourself first thing tomorrow. Right now, however, you've got other matters to which you must attend, comforting a crestfallen Andy not being the least of them.

You approach the boy from behind. You're mere inches away from that amber strip, the one you hold responsible for your forbidden fantasy. Squatting down, you

we are dna

move your mouth close to his ear. He no longer smells of a breath mint but rather a thick, aromatic, larger-than-life candy cane. You utter the words softly, gently.

"You really want to play this song, huh?"

He turns his head to the side, bats his eyelashes at you.

"You know what?" he grumbles. "It wouldn't bother me so much if I knew it was beyond my skill level, you know? Something I'm not yet prepared to tackle." His eyes burn into yours, his lean body so very determined.

"I can do this, Mr. Kuhn. I know I can." He lifts his head, twists his hips so that he is facing you.

"Show me how."

{

You've seen other teachers use this tactic before. That's how you know it safe, benign. One of your colleagues at Elmwood used to employ it regularly. At the time, you thought the activity unusual, indecent; you considered reporting it to your superior. Now, of course, you see the behavior differently.

"Okay, Andy. Now, I used to do this when I worked at Elmwood," you lie. "I found it to be rather effective. Let's just try it out once and see how it goes." You move in closer. "You don't mind my sitting almost on top of you, do you?" You breathe the words practically into the nape of his neck. "It's the only way this can really work."

"Hey, Mr. K, no problem," Andy says, scooting forward in order to allow you ample room. "You do whatever it takes. I don't get spooked easily." The boy never ceases to amaze you with how receptive he is to your every move, your every request. You wonder if for him there's even such a thing as "too close for comfort." You fantasize about just how close the two of you could be, how his body might receive yours wholly and completely.

For the time being, however, this is close enough. With your knees on opposite sides of the bench, you're now effectively straddling the student, your crotch coming into contact with the middle of his back. You draw your arms around him, a spider seizing its prey. You're in position. You begin instruction.

"Lay your hands on the keys, Andy." He does as you say. An obedient prey. "Now then, we're gonna start from the beginning and proceed all the way through. I want you to let my hands do all the work. The only thing that I request is that your hands give in entirely to mine. Don't resist my movements, the pressure of my fingers on yours. Relax your muscles and allow your hands to lie limp. Yes, just like that. I'll take them where they need to go. We can do this as many times as is necessary until you think you've got it, okay?"

we are dna

"Sounds good," the boy croaks, his voice cracking.

You wonder if he's really okay with this. His body seems relaxed but his throat, not so much. Somewhat conflicted, you decide to proceed, to make first contact. You spread your fingers, make a gentle landing first upon his knuckles then the whole of his hands. His skin is silky, decadently so. You worry that you'll have trouble keeping his fingers held captive under yours. Too easily could your hands leave his, pushing forward and away in rich, frictionless splendor. You must be careful, remain consciously aware of your every movement. You mustn't get lost in the moment. Your hands upon his the whole time. If you feel as though you're losing your grip or that you're gliding away, you'll simply pull your hands backward and nestle the boy once again under your wing. This isn't a simple task, but it can be done.

You once again coo into the boy's ear.

"We'll start slow until you get used to it." You take a deep breath and begin.

{

Keeping your hands on his is easier than you thought, especially once a fine layer of perspiration begins to form. When you initially feel the sweaty wetness under your skin, you fear it'll act as a lubricant, your molecular bond with the boy, if there even were such a thing, breaking apart. Instead it has the exact opposite effect. The salty secretions make your palms and the tops of his hands clammy, the juncture between the two sticky, muggy. In this way you play through the song three times, after which the heat, tension, and your passion alike combine together, becoming too unbearable to stand. You awkwardly excuse yourself, ripping your hands from the boy's. You waddle out of your office, into the hallway, and toward the bathroom. Your peculiar step delays physical explosion.

In the safety and relative privacy of the powder room, you undo your belt, allowing your pants—your underwear with them—to drop to the floor. You flop yourself onto the counter, align it with the center of the washbasin. You don't need to touch it, don't need to even look at it. Massaging would be superfluous. All you do is lift a hand, a sweaty hand, the perspiration not yours but Andy's, to your face. You inhale deeply. The effect is immediate.

Your body seiches violently, shudders as though it's malfunctioning. With a vague sense of nostalgia, your body feels not unlike a tire pump. An invisible handle is moving up and down; you can feel your muscles tightening, your blood pressurizing. It's all coming back to you. You clench your jaw and rest your head on the vanity's mirror. With your eyes closed, the scent of Andy—his body, his pheromones—overpowering your senses, you brace your

we are dna

body for occupant evacuation. The exodus is as epic as it is rapturous, a once-in-a-lifetime experience, something to which, in a free-love society, a TV miniseries would be devoted. It is like nothing you've ever known.

When you return to your study, the boy is no longer at the piano but instead bent, in what appears to be mourning, over your desk. You quickly realize that he can't possibly be crying; there's a fiendish grin on his face. Okay, so he's delighting in something, but what? As you move closer, his source of interest grows apparent. Clutched there, between his brawny fingers, is one of your many desktop picture frames. The frame itself is of a murky pewter, its surface polished but not overtly so. You've always favored that frame, the way it can reflect light and yet still retain its inner darkness. Housed inside is one of your and Tabitha's many wedding portraits (a posed embrace, the two of you pretending to smile). The photo and the frame complement one another nicely. Your marriage, just like the shape-shifting, at once dark yet light picture frame, is a quintessential paradox. Turn it, tilt it, view it any way you like, it'll never make much sense.

You stand behind the boy and casually peer over his shoulder. He looks up at you, his face beaming.

"Wow, you two really love each other." He flashes you a lopsided smile, is genuinely touched.

"Oh? And just what makes you say that?" You desperately want to undermine the boy's confidence, force him to doubt his assertion, retract that ugly statement. He needs to know, needs to fully understand that your heart has no bonds and no ties, that it is entirely his. You'll take whatever measures are necessary to convey this.

"I dunno. I mean, God, it's everything—the way you're smiling, holding her hand; the way she's laughing, how she has her hands around your waist. Everything about this, man, just screams love."

You steal the picture frame from out of his hands and return it to the desk facedown. You look him straight in the eye.

"Andrew, if there were one thing I could teach you, one thing I could get you to understand, to always remember, it wouldn't be a finger placement or a melody. It'd be this: My dear boy, not everything is as it seems." You squeeze his shoulder in an effort to lighten the mood. "I want to give you something."

Returning to the piano, you squat down and flip open the lid of the bench. There's a rustling of papers as you jostle about the songbooks, the saddle-stitched binders in search of a particular piece, a very specific document. You locate it near the bottom. It is an eight-page composition, its melody and harmony handwritten. Its notes were plotted not by a computer but by hand in dark ink. You hold it out to the boy.

we are dna

"What is this?" he asks. "It looks ... complicated."

"It's just a little something that I'd like you to work on in your free time," you explain, "something to do when your lacrosse buddies are ... uh ... well, doing whatever it is that they do when not playing lacrosse." You smile weakly. There are puddles of sweat forming in your underarms.

"Huh, all right. I'll give it a try." He lifts his eyes from the document. "Who wrote it?"

Your face reddens. You dig your toes into the carpet.

"Uh ... well ... me. I-I-I w-wrote it." You feel like a blundering idiot, your speech broken, lame. The boy, however, pays little attention to your eloquence or, in this case, your lack thereof. He's more concerned with what you have to say than how you say it. You're grateful for that.

"No way, dude! Are you effing serious?!" The whiteness of his teeth contrasts sharply with the darkness of his gaping mouth.

"Yeah," you confess, nodding your head, "I get a little embarrassed about it. I wrote it after grad school. I ... I've never asked anyone else to play it before."

You look up at him. He's the one, the only one. You must make that clear.

"Man, what an accomplishment! Dude, I've never known a composer before! This is awesome." He's flipping through the music again, his feet gleefully bouncing up and down. He's making much too light of the situation. If only he would calm down, he could maybe comprehend the gravity of the situation, the weight of the gesture. This is a serious gift, something you haven't given to anyone ever before, not even Tabitha. This is not just any old packet of piano music. No, this is *your* music, your story, your very life force on a platter.

The boy has an inquisitive look on his face.

"Well, Mr. K, I really can't wait to practice this. I mean, jeez, it's always a good sign when a quick sight-read like this gets me all stirred up. There's one thing I don't get, though. What's with the title? 'We R DNA, Pots Raven'?"

He bites his lip. "What does that even mean?"

"It's actually a fairly long story," you say, your eyes on the clock. It's 3:45 PM. You haven't much time. Mrs. McMillon will be in your yard bowling for briars any minute now. You close the bench and plop yourself down on its cushion. The sheer heft of your ass sends a cloud of dust exploding into the air.

The boy tosses a grimace your way.

"Oh, no, the man is sitting down," he groans with mock annoyance. "I better go unfold a blanket and find myself a pillow." He tries to suppress it, but he can't; a smile sprawls across his face. "It's gonna be a long after-

we are dna

noon."

With your socked foot you give his knee a playful kick. He's so goddamned charming, you can't stand it. It's as if cuteness has been hardwired into him or something. Never before have you fallen for someone this innately captivating, this intrinsically lovable. Then again, never before have you fallen for a man or, rather, a boy. You wonder what he'll look like when he grows up, when he reaches adulthood. Would the allure remain, diminish, or grow stronger? You hope that you'll be there to find out, not as a distant friend, an auxiliary acquaintance but rather as a counselor, a confidant—the one who makes him laugh, smile, and sing, maybe even moan.

You send him a grin hungrier than it is happy. "I'll give you the abridged version of the story, okay?"

"Yeah, like, whatever. I'm waiting." He lifts his hand and flops it around, assumes a Valley Girl accent as bitchy as it is brainless.

"All right, listen up, you airhead," you tease, launching into your story. "It goes something like this."

ʡ

When finishing up your graduate work at the University of Akron, you opted to live on campus and become a resident assistant for its single but oh so worthwhile perk—

free room and board. You agreed to the position under the assumption that you'd be assigned a single, that your room would be devoid of chatterboxes, kept kleptomaniac-free. You had done the whole roommate thing once before, as an undergraduate. You'd rather kill your mother than go through that again. Needless to say, when you arrived at your dorm and saw two names on the door, you quickly retracted the statement.

Your roommate was an Indian man, an aspiring chemist, the one who you'd come to call Pots Raven. That wasn't his name, of course. Though he was born in the States, his parents were not, and although he was a first-generation American, his parents were hell-bent on his never becoming "American." He wouldn't become like one of those Chinese or Arab children about which they had heard such terrible things, things like their being ashamed of their heritage. Whenever friends, colleagues, heck, even the occasional dental assistant would call his name, Paritosh Revaji, he'd hear not only the syllables, the speech sounds, but so much more; he'd hear the call, the cry of his homeland. At least that was the plan.

By the time he reached middle school, no one called him Paritosh, much less thought that his name. He was Pots, the nickname given to him by some lazy-tongued kids back in third grade. At the time he thought the moniker temporary. He figured that he'd lose it within the year.

we are dna

He was wrong. Twenty years later, he'd find himself shaking your hand, welcoming you to Akron, telling you to call him Pots. You'd ask for his last name. He'd pause, ruminate for a moment. "Raven," he'd say. "My name is Pots Raven."

You shared a room, shared a life with Paritosh "Pots Raven" Revaji for two full years. Neither of you went home for the holidays, not for Christmas, not for Ganesh Chaturthi. Instead, both of you remained in Akron, became interim recluses, relished in little else than one another's company.

Pots Raven was a self-professed philosophile, a man who delighted in all things existential. Late at night, when the sky would fall empty, turn godless, you would hear him speak. The words were always soft, almost inaudible. "What are we?" Sometimes you'd hear nothing at all. Those were the nights during which he'd merely mouth the words, his body too tired, too wearied to produce voice.

On your graduation day he was the first person that you hugged, the only person you had wanted to hug. He held your face in his hands and told you that you were his best friend, that he was immensely proud of you. Two weeks later you wrote the song. It came to you quickly, took little more time to pen than it does to play. When you were finished, you smiled to yourself. You had an answer to Pots Raven's midnight question; you had a title for your piece.

{

Andrew waits a while before speaking. His silence seems not so much out of reverence but, rather, anticipation. He fears that you might yet have more to say, that his feedback would somehow break your train of thought. He allows you thirty seconds or so to resume your storytelling, but when you say no more, when your lips stay still, he figures it safe and takes his turn.

"Dang, man, that's really deep … and here I thought you were nothing more than some fast-moving fingers." There's a naughty grin on his face. His boyish lips are redder than usual. You contemplate in what other situations he might make that face, after what other endeavors his lips might flush. You'd do terrible things, unspeakable things for the opportunity to find out. Your desperation is palpable, damn near visible. It scares you; you scare you.

The boy is by the window now. He appears to be checking for his mother, that or perhaps his own reflection; you're not sure which. In a perfect world, or at least, *your* perfect world, one without boundaries and limitations, where intimacy with a minor is not a crime, things would be different—gloriously different. Andy would still be at the window, sure, but he would not be alone—not for long,

we are dna

anyway. You'd slink up behind him, holding your breath, stilling your heartbeat. Your hands would blind his eyes and your lips descend, mere feathers upon his ear. You'd speak in a tone that is gentle, breathe a directive that is firm. The words would enter his ears like music, tear through him like knives. He'd think that he misheard you and request that you reiterate. You'd look him dead in the eye, your hands outstretched. You'd slowly, confidently repeat the words.

Don't scream.

Before your meaning could register, before his mind could comprehend, your hands would have his collar. The cotton would feel cool, its weave tight, soft. You'd know then that it'd have to go, that it must be destroyed. If you were going to do this, you were going to do it right. Nothing on the boy would remain cool, stay soft.

One quick, concerted jerk is all it would take. The shirt, torn open, would hit the floor. Next would be the pants, those tight, restrictive pants. Something, a prisoner, would be pushing, prodding at the zippered door. A sense of duty would compel you, and you'd take appropriate action. Around the boy's knees the pants would drop. The briefs underneath would be both low-rise and low-cut; they would cling to his groin; they would hide little else.

By this time you would have beheld just about ninety percent of the boy's flesh. If you were back in the classroom and that number were a test score, you'd represent it not as a percentage but as a fraction. It would be a 90/100 or, simplified, a 9/10. On a standardized grading scale, that'd equate to a B+. It wouldn't be good enough. Andy is a high-performing student and you an exceptional educator; both of you would deserve better, would deserve that perfect one hundred percent. Besides, good students deserve good rewards. You'd have a gold star for the boy and would know exactly where to put it. The briefs would pose little threat. When you'd hit their elastic band, when you'd be facing down their very defenses, you'd do only that which feels natural. You would go subterranean; you would get lost in the trenches.

"Uh oh, a red car. It's coming around the corner ... is slowing ... stopping ... yep, it's her." He turns around, faces you. He's fully dressed. His mouth is pouting. "That's my cue to go, Mr. K."

You have no idea what he's talking about. Blinking your eyes, you look about the room. *Oh, my God*, your soul cries. *It never happened. The shirt, the pants, the red briefs— none of it.* You second-guess the logic, are disbelieving. *No, it can't be. I smothered him with my touch. My hands were on his ... his everything.* You'll prove it to yourself. The boy smells of peppermint. If your hands did as you say, then they should too.

You touch your fingers to the flap of skin between

we are dna

your nose and mouth. It's your gesture of contemplation, one to which the boy is accustomed. Solemnly, hopefully, you expand your lungs. What you want is the scent of a red-and-white-striped candy. What you get is a whiff of metal, the odor of pennies. You feel a fool, a self-deceiving, borderline schizophrenic fool. You never clutched the boy. The last thing to leave an impression was a pewter picture frame, a fetid one at that. You visualize the wedding portrait and shudder.

Releasing a thick, sorrowful sigh, you lock eyes with the boy. "There was something I was going to tell you," you lie. "I was trying to think of it just now, but eh, I can't remember. Mustn't have been important." You hope that he falls for the poorly concocted lie but doubt that he will.

The boy doesn't seem to be listening. His eyes are on your score, his feet shuffling their way out of the office. You trail closely behind, a dog hungry for affection. As you reach the vestibule, your attention pulls back from the boy and up toward the ceiling. The chandelier, which should be still, at rest, is swinging about noisily. Its chain is yearning for oil, is squeaking its way back and forth above your head. You look around the room. Nothing else appears unsettled, disturbed. Your valuables are just as they were—thrown atop display case shelves, grayed with dust, forgotten. The front door's deadbolt is flipped in the locked position. There's no other movement in the house, no wailing floorboards, no shuffling of feet. All seems well.

If for nothing else but your own peace of mind, you peek into the adjacent dining room and examine its expensive but largely unused fixtures. The toffee-colored beechwood chairs. The similarly styled hardwood table. Its yellowed doily, a Belgian original from Tabitha and Daddy Dukes with love. The hutch with its aged rippled glass. The once plush, now passé, shag carpet. The long-handled feather duster, ideal for getting to those hard-to-reach places.

Wait a minute. That doesn't belong here. Why is the feather duster in the dining room rather than—it clicks. Tabitha must have been cleaning the chandelier. Yes, that must be it. She was in here. Recently. No, mere seconds ago. You feel a twisting of your stomach, a knotting of the bile-rich chambers. *Why did she feel the need to scurry away? She was out here, poking at the chandelier with that damn stick when she heard our approach. Something—maybe a feeling, an intuition—sent her fleeing first into the dining room, then away. What could it have been? What was that "something"?*

"Mr. Kuhn, is everything all right?" The boy is balancing on one foot, craning his neck to get a look at what has so fully captured your attention. He appears concerned.

"Yeah, yeah," you reassure, retreating back toward the

we are dna

boy, toward the one who has reinvigorated your spirit, made your otherwise squalid life worth living. He is the one who would, in your perfect world, have Tabitha's ring on his finger. "Tabitha was in here recently is all. I'm not sure why she left so quickly, so I was just checking to see if maybe she was in the dining room."

The boy is puzzled.

"Tabitha? Tabitha who? Is that another one of your students?" His words are accusatory and seem a tinge bitter. You laugh.

"No, no, you silly boy!" You run a hand through his tousled hair, stirring the modern-day Minthe who lives inside. "Tabitha is my wife. You know, Mrs. Kuhn? I seldom slip up and call her by her first name in front of students ... that is, except for you. I always want to call her 'Tabitha' when talking to you."

The boy doesn't get it. He scratches his head.

"Why?"

You don't really want to explain. You don't even know if you can. Still, in Andrew's eyes, beyond the confusion, the incomprehension, lies intrigue. Even if you don't want to tell, he wants to know. You'll do it for him, only for him. You'll try to put into words what has so long been a private emotion.

"I ... well ... to be honest, I don't really know why, Andy." You clear your throat. "There are so many differences between us—hundreds, really, hell, even millions—but when we're together, they seem irrelevant or, rather, inconsequential. I dunno, I guess I just know that there's a special bond here, something so few people are lucky enough to experience, to cherish, you know? You're not so much a student to me as … God, I dunno. Suffice it to say you're a lot more than a check for thirty dollars, okay?"

Your eyes are on the floor. You fail to see the smile upon the boy's face, the way in which his body language has changed, how receptive he has become, how he's moving closer, closer, how he's now against you, his arms around your waist, how he's pulling tightly, how he's hugging you like a son, a friend, a lover.

You feel what has become a frequent friction in your pants. The boy's arms aren't releasing their grip but, rather, are pulling tighter, bringing the two of you closer. You can feel yourself throbbing against the boy's lower abdomen. The pulsation is strong. You wonder, worry about whether he can feel it. You kind of hope he can.

The boy is lifting his head, his eyes upturned toward yours. His lips are wet, his fragrance unrelentingly sweet. The words are soft.

"You're a good guy, Mr. K. I knew that the moment I met you. But now I feel like I should say something else." He pauses. "You're a good friend, Mr. K." His fingers dance upon your back, draw swirls, and—wait—was

we are dna

that a heart just now? He pulls you tight for just a moment longer before letting you go, letting his hands fall to his sides. He turns, and before you know it, he's out the door with filthy running shoes in one hand, "We R DNA" in the other. You shut the front doors and, without a moment's deliberation, race to the nearby powder room.

A careless whip of your wrist sends the cell's door slamming shut. For the second time in one day, you undo your belt, lower your pants. With a clear objective in mind, you begin your work. To be honest, it's not as enjoyable an activity as you had expected it to be. Having done something markedly similar just twenty minutes prior, the gesture feels tired, tedious even. Still, you proceed onward, strong in your conviction that with proper stimulation and the right Andrew-centric visions, anything is possible. To you, this is not just a theory; it's a time-tested reality. You believe in its existence almost as much as you reject that of God's.

Needless to say, you are not surprised when your hypothesis is once again confirmed, when your body defies your early expectations and, against all odds, performs without malfunction. As you rear back in preparation for release, you open your mouth and scream out the only name that comes to mind. He is suddenly there before you, ready and willing to take direction, to adhere to your every request. In telling this imaginary Andrew what to

brian lucas

do, you issue the most lewd and ribald of commands. It's not enough to merely think the words; no, you want to—you *need* to—say them out loud, to hear them exit your mouth amidst the chaos of your hectic breath. The words, their arrangements, both are some of the nastiest in the English language. You don't care. You love the filthiness of your fantasies, the grossness of your groans. That which is indecent you make explicit; what is distasteful you render repulsive. Every utterance, every remark is pushed over and beyond its limits. Your sentiments are not just off-color; they are off-grayscale, off-sepia—hell—off the goddamn visual spectrum. Inside of the room, you are howling, convulsing, indulging in a fantasy of which you'll never tire. Outside of the room, Tabitha is listening, trembling, anticipating the moment in which she'll reveal to you all that she has heard.

The remainder of the day dies quickly. Its night, however, lasts for what seems a lifetime. It's 7:30 PM. You're walking about the house, securing your and Tabitha's privacy by way of closing the blinds, drawing the curtains. It's a ritualized activity, one to which you've been assigned. Tabitha greets the morning, opens the house. You, in turn, flout the evening, refuse its entry. Like so many of your domestic chores, this too is brainless. You move from window to window, pulling strings, yanking curtains, and clamping drapes. Yes, that's right: clamping. When Tabitha says, "Close the curtains," she means it. We're not talking about a simple overlapping of the fabric; we're talking the alignment of the drapes edge to edge and the literal fastening of them together.

A wise man or, in this case, woman would have

stitched some sort of device into the cloth, would have interwoven, say, a button or a pin. Hell, even Velcro appliqués would do the trick. Tabitha contends that she was never given "adequate time" to envision and integrate such a gadget. Besides, she would snort, why make such elaborate accommodations when you've got ample paperclips at your disposal?

You didn't waste your time with a secondary appeal. Tabitha had spoken; paperclipping would be the remedy of choice. And from that day forward it has been. For decades now, you've spent every night at the house's windows, installing paperclips between what always seem far too many sets of drapes. Tonight is no different. You've already clipped the bedrooms and the master bath. You're en route to the living room when the obstruction that is Tabitha's body blocks your passage. Against the door frame she is leaning, her eyes lowered, hands clenched into fists. You detect in her an energy, a passion which you believed had died long ago. Although you can't see her eyes, her lashes remain visible. They are fluttering in and out of view; she is blinking back tears.

"Tabitha?"

Your voice is weak, faltering. You grunt your throat clear, then try again. "Tabitha? Are you okay?" Her blinking stops. "What's going on?"

Slowly, almost imperceptibly, she lifts her head. Her

we are dna

skin is so white that it borders on blue. She has the distinct look of the living dead. Her eyes are closed; her head is shaking.

"And all of this time," she begins, her voice hoarse, "I had thought that you had wanted to be some sort of father figure to him." Her lips are trembling; her hair is wet. She must have just recently taken a shower. With a spasmodic batting of her lashes, her eyes open and meet yours. They are beyond bloodshot, are borderline bleeding. "What a fool you took me for, and worse, what a fool I was." She turns away from you, trudges into the darkened living room. There, without lifting a hand to a lamp, does she fall to the floor, collapse into a heap. You follow after her, but with caution, trepidation. Outside, the wind is rattling against the unsheathed panes. Gusts are howling through the nearby woods, through the darkness of the night's oblivion.

"Tabitha, what is this all about? What's going on? I don't under—"

"Mr. Kuhn," she interrupts, "you listen to me, and you listen well." Though you cannot see her, see anything, you know with absolute certainty that her eyes are on you. You can feel the hate. "Are you listening?" The words are soft, unnervingly so.

"Yes, Tabitha, I'm listening."

"Good. Then hear this: Don't fuck with me."

brian lucas

Her turn-of-the-century haughtiness, her decades-old language, the archaic grammar—all of it is gone. This is Tabitha in her pure, undiluted, unrehearsed form. This is a woman whose longstanding habituations are gone, who is at her basest level, who is raw. As she continues to rage, her diction is exaggerated to an almost violent degree. Her s's are scathing hisses, her t's furious exhalations. This intensity in her voice is something that you've never heard before, something that you didn't even think existed—at least, not in her.

"I heard you in the bathroom this afternoon, Harold. Don't do yourself the disservice of trying to deny me this. You're caught, okay? Do you hear me? You're caught! The game is over."

Your heart is beating frantically. Though you're disturbed by the pitilessness of her wrath, the assertiveness in her accusations, you're interested to see where this is going.

"Tab, I ... I don't know what to say. I'll tell you anything, everything you want. Please, Tab, just listen—"

"Tab? Tab! Hm, I almost forgot about that one, Harold. Leave it to you to call up a dead pet name in times of distress. What do you think, that you can summon up some forty-year-old term of endearment and have me eating out of your palm just like that? For being a teacher, a goddamn piano prodigy, you sure can be a fucking idiot. 'Tab' isn't gonna make me forget the fact that you want to

we are dna

fool around with a boy who might very well still sleep with a blankie. Then again, what do I know? Knowing you, you've probably already tried something."

Your wife's complexion, once snowy, now appears ashen. It's as if there had been a flame inside of her that had been snuffed out, its smoke having penetrated her face and settled there. Beads of perspiration bedeck her forehead; her eyebrows are soggy. Her skin is no longer a cluster of cells but a nation of goose bumps.

"Tabitha, honey, are you feeling all right? You look as though you might—"

"Aren't you straight, Harold?" she blurts. "Isn't that why you married me? You wanted to be with a woman? Sure seemed that way at the time, what with your telling me how you wanted to do this or that, plant your face here or there. You and your sordid fantasies. I should have known something was wrong then, the way you'd wax so sexual. But, hell, at least it was about a girl. Can't say I had thought you would one day be talking about a man, let alone a fifteen-year-old boy. You do know he's underage, don't you? That your gay yearnings are not only that but also illegal? They could hang you high for those fucking vulgar musings."

"Tabitha, I know," you say, dropping to the floor beside her. "I know that it's not okay, but ... well, it is what it is."

brian lucas

"Oh, my God," soars Tabitha, her voice an octave higher than usual, "did I hear you correctly? Did Mr. Kuhn, the glorious, fucking infallible Mr. Kuhn actually admit blame?! No, surely I must have heard him wrong. What was that, Mr. Kuhn? Say it one more time, loud enough so that everyone can hear."

"Tabitha, stop it. Please."

"No!" she rebuffs. "I want to hear you fucking say it. Go on, Harold. Say it. 'I like little boys.'"

"Tabitha, no! It's not about the age, the gender, the anything. I don't like boys; I just … happen to like An—"

"Say it, you pedophilic fucker! Scream it, mean it! 'I like fucking little boys.' Go on, you rat-bastard! Tell me about your screwy predilection!"

"Tabitha, stop! I'm not going to say it because it is not—"

"You're a coward! A goddamned coward." Her arm twists at the elbow; her fist slams into your chest. "Go on, boy-hunter, you tell me; what is it that you want from him, huh? His body? His undeveloped muscle? His baby fat? No? None of those? Oh, I know. What about his virgin penis, huh? You wanna—what—touch it to yours? Compare their sizes? See if they work the same? Hey, maybe you can figure out a way to persuade his into liking yours! That might be fun! So what if yours is covered in spider-veins and his is a pristine pink? Everyone likes a little vari-

we are dna

ety, right?"

"Tabitha!" you roar, no longer willing to play victim to her verbal assaults, "that's more than enough! How dare you say such vicious things and to your husband, no less! My God, you should be ashamed of yourself! I know that I've done wrong, but Jesus, I want to reform myself; I want to do right!" You're out of air and gasping for breath. "Let me do right!"

Out from the fibers of the carpet come the sounds of muted sobs. Tabitha's head is down on the floor, her tears darkening the throw carpet's Persian designs. Her weeping is delirious and sounds painful. She begins to choke on her tears, the ever-thickening phlegm in her throat. This too sounds painful.

"You might want to get me a trash can," she says, her hacking unabated. "I think I might vomit."

You lay a hand on her upper back. "It's okay," you say. "I can clean it up." Wordlessly, the two of you sit, one struggling to breathe, the other grappling with emotions too complicated to explain. Neither of you feels good; neither of your circumstances is even remotely enviable. Bound in space and time by destinies not of your own choosing, there's little to do but sit and wait. In time the coughing relents.

"We've always lived separate lives, Harold," Tabitha breathes, her voice weak, throat scratchy. "I never thought that to be an innately bad thing. Sure, there was room for improvement, but ... I mean, we had our routines, our schedules, our dissimilar interests. I thought it was healthy to pursue that which brings you happiness, thought it only natural that different interests meant different walks of life." She breathes in deeply and lets out a short burst of air. "I guess I never thought that one of our separate paths would lead us astray or ... could jeopardize all that we have." Her hand alights on yours. The skin is dry, old, chafed. "You know as well as I that we can't go on like this, Harold. You've got to stop the piano lessons now, today. You must never again see that boy. Do you understand me?"

Your head is nodding. "T-tabitha, I'm s-so s-s-sorry," you stammer. "I know what you are s-s-saying b-but I ... I don't know if I c-can do it. I know i-it's right to s-stop seeing the boy, b-but I d-d-don't know if m-my body will let me." Feeling a failure, you expel a sigh, retch forth the truth. "I *know* m-m-my body won't let me."

You feel a hand brush through your hair. The physical contact is soothing.

"Poor Mr. Kuhn," says a seemingly sympathetic Tabitha, "you look a mess, babe. Don't you worry that silly little head of yours for another moment. Mrs. Kuhn will make everything all right." Unexpectedly, she pulls her hand from yours. "For the sake of her own well-being,

we are dna

Mrs. Kuhn has gotta make everything all right."

You don't like the intentional ambiguity of this declaration, this potentially misguided mission statement. You're in desperate need of elaboration.

"What do you mean?" you ask. "What are you going to do?"

Mrs. Kuhn stands up, brushing off whatever may or may not have settled upon her dress. She looks down at you. It's from this newfound position of authority that she speaks.

"Sweetheart, don't you get it by now? What you've done, what you've intended to do, has left stains on my conscience. Sorry to say, but you don't exist in a vacuum. Your actions, your frenzied, illogical impulses, they have an impact. In this case they primarily affected the boy. Really, all I got was the aftershock." As if by instinct, she begins to fluff her hair, correct her damaged appearance. "Unfortunately for you, these particular aftershocks were significant enough to register on the Richter scale. I'm sorry, babe, but I can't just let this go." She looses a silent yawn.

"For thirty-six years now, I've lived, moved, and slept with a man who, by this experience, has shown himself a stranger and, by God, an ugly one at that. Now, since I'm not an impulsive person, I won't be doing anything tonight—that is, other than sleeping. Come morning's light,

brian lucas

I ... well, frankly, I don't know what I'll do. I guess whatever feels right. You can rest assured that I'll be making a call to the McMillon house, that I'll be talking with Aubrey and Andrew. Because your word is as good as shit, I'll need to hear it from the boy that he's okay, that you've never laid your geriatric hands upon him. After that"—she shrugs—"you've got me. Maybe I'll call the police, maybe my lawyer. I don't know, Harold. I just don't know."

She turns to go but, before she does, changes her mind. Standing only inches away from you, she squats down and lifts your chin so that her eyes may meet yours. Despite the darkness, you discern a weak smile upon her face. Lowering a hand to the ground, she leans forward; she gives you one last kiss upon the forehead. Her mouth is now upon your ear, the words airy but aloof.

"My dear Harold, you are not well."

With that she rises, turns, and, without a second glance, leaves you to your solitude.

﹛

You wait two hours before trying the stairs, before attempting an infiltration of the bedroom. Tabitha needs to be asleep, deeply asleep. You can't risk her waking up. Seeing as the both of you suffered a tumultuous night, you assume that she'll require a full hour—as opposed to her

we are dna

usual fifteen minutes—to fall unconscious. You've decided to see that one hour and raise it to two, the notion being that only an insomniac could resist sleep for such a duration. Tabitha is known countywide for her ability to sleep hard and to sleep fast. She is rumored to have never seen the ending of a movie, to have never observed the leisurely rise of a film's credits. You should, for all intents and purposes, have nothing to worry about.

Your trek through the master bedroom and into the bath goes off without a hitch, without so much as a mindless muttering from your unconscious wife. You take a deep breath, secure in the knowledge that it's all downhill from here. In just a few minutes' time, it'll be over; it'll all be over. No awkward explanations, no inappropriate impulses, no humiliating declarations. The recent past will all be but a bubble, blown out and away from the dipping pan of your life. The small, translucent sphere will float low to the ground, flouncing this way and that, according to the wind's direction. Strangely adverse to the idea of bursting, the bubble will defy the sharp grass's expectations, will dip low only to then rebound and soar higher and farther than ever before. This process will repeat several carefree times prior to catching a predator's eye. Once caught in the aiming reticle, once identified as a target, the bubble hasn't long to live; its whirls are numbered. One single, timely clap is all it will take. Two hands will meet, there'll be a pop, a slap, and the bubble will be gone. On the hands of the predator will be a residue, a quickly drying, fast evaporating solution. Moments ago there was a bubble; now there is a goo; moments later there'll be nothing.

You open a cabinet under the sink marked "TK." Inside are dozens upon dozens of bottles, hundreds of them, their respective perfumes and body scrubs too aromatic for Mrs. Kuhn in her delicate condition. Last winter Tabitha was the ungrateful recipient of one such product, a syrupy ooze which, when applied topically, was purported to dull headaches. You're able to remember this unremarkable gifting as it was initiated by Rachelle, your perpetually considerate student who "couldn't help" buying Tabitha a Christmas present. The unappreciated oil was housed in a green vial. Now if only you could remember the shape and design of its cap. It wasn't floral, wasn't especially ornate, definitely wasn't medicinal. What did it look like?

Just then you see it. The cylindrical bottle is at the very back of the unit, sandwiched between a Parisian perfume (anniversary gift) and an irregularly shaped body lotion (Happy New Year!). You lift it up and out of the cabinet and, holding it in your hand, examine its label.

we are dna

SAINT WINTERMINT'S CHEER

Seasonally Inspired Scent,
Everyday Pain Relief.

FOR TOPICAL USE ONLY   50 mL (1.69 US FL OZ)

Untwisting the cap, you draw the bottle toward your face. As you were instructed in science class some forty-five years earlier, you don't inhale the vapors directly but rather waft them in the general direction of your nose. The scent enters your lungs hard and strong. The elixir's fragrance, though never before sampled and artificially reproduced, is oddly familiar, stimulating even.

You close your eyes and take a second whiff, this one straight from the bottle. Although this causes the membranes of your nose to burn, you're indifferent to the pain. All you can see, all you can hear, all you can smell is Andrew. He's there with you in the bathroom, climbing up on the counter, shimmying his way over to and in front of you. His intoxicating aroma makes your knees weak, your mind manic. You can barely breathe, can hardly keep yourself upright. He's everything and nothing, everywhere and nowhere. He wants to be with you now, forever. You tell him that he's not alone in feeling this way, that the craving is reciprocated. He is smiling, is asking you if you know what you must do. You tell him "yes," ask him to go for a moment, to return when summoned. He tells you that he'll be waiting, that this is it, this is the moment, your moment.

Opening your eyes, you turn the vial around and scrutinize the almost illegibly small text on its back. You're not disappointed by what you see.

WARNING: FOR TOPICAL USE ONLY. BALM CONTAINS A HIGH CONCENTRATION OF PENNYROYAL, AN ESSENTIAL OIL RICH IN PULEGONE. NOT FOR USE ON PREGNANT WOMEN. FATAL IF SWALLOWED.

Your eyes are once again shut. Andrew has kept his promise, is once again seated on the counter before you. His eyes are sparkling, his grin infectious. Standing alone in the bathroom, you face the mirror, your mouth curled into a smile. The boy's arms are around you now; you're sweating from the heat of his love. "Don't worry about what will happen," he reassures. "Everything will be all right." His eyes are on yours. "What are you waiting for, Mr. K? We're more than DNA, aren't we?"

we are dna

You nod your head slowly and surely. Your mouth opens; you tell your teeth to hold the bottle in place. You tell your body, your mind that there's nothing to fear, that they won't feel a thing. Andrew is tugging on your shirt, is diverting your attention.

"Tell me, Mr. K," he pleads. "Tell me that this isn't the end, that there's more to enjoy, more to experience. Tell me we are more than DNA."

"Kid," you say, "you better believe it."

In one swift motion, your head tips back, your throat downs the syrup, and your teeth drop the vial. The glass bottle shatters on the floor. A neuron or two fires, a muscle or two twitches, then nothing.

Then everything.

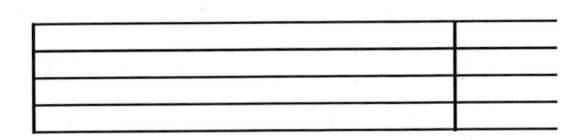

The McMillon household receives its mail at twelve noon every day, rain or shine, sleet or hail. Saturday, October 24, is no different. Mrs. McMillon collects the mail at exactly 12:16 PM. Four envelopes, no parcels. They are reviewed on the kitchen counter. Bill. Reminder notice from the veterinarian. Advertisement addressed to "Current Resident." Card addressed to Andrew McMillon. Andrew receives the letter at 12:19 PM. On the front of the greeting card is a photo of a grand piano in sepia tone. On the inside are twelve lines of handwritten text. They read:

Andrew
Im sorry for lying to you. Though I did indeed write We R DNA just

> after college I never titled the piece. Not until recently anyway. Though I roomed with an Indian friend during college his name was not Pots Raven. Do you remember what I told you during our last lesson?
> Nothing is what it seems.
> HK

The correspondence did not immediately make sense to Andrew. In fact, it took him several hours to understand its significance. If Mr. Kuhn never knew a Pots Raven, then why would he use that name? Then again, it's not really a name. It's more like an incoherent pairing of words, a seemingly nonsensical jumbling of letters.

This was his moment of epiphany. Pots Raven only *seemed* a jumbling of letters. In reality, it was something much more. The boy took out a sheet of notebook paper and, in big block letters, scrawled the title of Mr. Kuhn's overture.

WE R DNA, POTS RAVEN

we are dna

He removed the punctuation, disregarded the spaces.

WERDNAPOTSRAVEN

And that was when he saw it, when he finally decrypted the message. The composition's title itself meant nothing, was little more than a strategic placement of letters. In reversing those letters, however, Andrew found what was lost. The sentence was a simple instruction; the words were Mr. Kuhn's last.

NEVARSTOPANDREW
NEVAR STOP, ANDREW

NEVER STOP, ANDREW.

And he never did. Oh, sure, he gave up the piano just a year later. It turned out it wasn't his thing. Yeah, he was good—talented even—but oh, well. There were other hobbies, other activities in which he engaged. When he graduated high school, he moved to Spain for a year to study Spanish. After that came Mexico, Argentina, and Xavier University. He graduated with an undergraduate degree in Spanish language and was encouraged to pursue his master's and doctorate. He said that he'd think about it

brian lucas

but knew that he wouldn't. He didn't belong in a classroom, a stuffy hall bloated with under-qualified professors and overzealous pupils. He'd get his education from other places, from surfing the world's seascapes or from climbing its equally formidable cityscapes. Life was full of possibilities. He would never stop❋